# Key to a Murder

*An Antique Hunters Mystery Book 4*

by

Vicki Vass

For information, email **Vicki Vass**, vicki@vickivass.com  or visit our website at: vickivass.com

ISBN: 978-0-9989893-4-1

Printed in the United States of America

Cover design by Paula Ellenberger
http://www.paulaellenberger.com

1 2 3 4 5 6 7 8 9 10

## Dedication

To Bandit "Boo-Boo Bear" Tedeschi, more than a companion. A hero in my stories and my life.
(2003-2016)

Special thanks to Corinna Petry whose talent as a writer and editor always makes me a better storyteller.

Chapter One

"Help me," a voice called, piercing through the rain and thunder. The doorknob twisted frantically matching the urgency of the late-night caller. "Please," the voice pleaded.

Anne ran from the back room to the front door, unlatching it. Standing in front of her was an elderly woman holding an old lantern. She was wrapped in a worn hooded yellow raincoat. Her soft red hair was speckled with gray; her face weathered from age; her once bright blue eyes fading to a watery pale blue. When she saw Anne, those eyes glimmered with hope. With a heavy moan, the woman collapsed into Anne's arms.

Anne pulled her into the store and placed her on an antique Victorian fainting couch. *Appropriate for the occasion,* Anne thought. "Are you okay?" Anne asked.

The woman blinked her eyes. She moved her lips but no words came out.

Anne pulled out her phone to dial 9-1-1. The woman grabbed her arm with a strength Anne wouldn't have believed she had. "Please don't call the police." Her breathing was labored, her words slurred.

"What's wrong? Tell me what's wrong."

"Water. Can I have some water please?"

Anne ran to the kitchenette and came back carrying a bottle of water. The woman sat up on the couch and took a long drink. Anne pulled up a small stool and sat across from her. As she did, the woman let out a low moan and fell back into the couch. Her raincoat flung open, her white cotton blouse was drenched, not from the rain, but from blood pouring from a stab wound. With a shaky hand, she handed Anne the lantern and then she was gone.

From behind the front counter, Aunt Sybil watched in silence as Anne did her best to revive the poor woman but, like Aunt Sybil, the woman was dead. Anne had seen enough dead bodies to know that her damages were beyond repair. No coming back from that conclusion. Anne called the police—well, she called *her* police, Chicago Detective Nigel Towers. He would know what to do. Anne carefully laid the old woman onto the couch before covering her with a patchwork quilt. She tucked the edges around her. A bloody piece of paper fell out of her raincoat pocket. Anne carefully unfolded it to see an article from the *Guardian*, a British daily newspaper. She was familiar with it thanks to her best friend, CC. The headline read, "Spoon Sisters Solve Estate Sale Murders in U.S."

"Ohmigosh, we're world famous," Anne said out loud then regretted the pleasure it gave her considering the fate of its messenger. She read the story, which had been picked up from the *Chicago Tribune* wire service and then embellished by local reporters: "Liverpool-born Detective Nigel Towers, now with the Chicago Police Department, helped break the murder spree in Chicago's wealthy North Shore suburbs. Detective Towers' father, the legendary Reginald Towers of Scotland Yard, was killed in the line of duty when Nigel was 12. He and his mother moved to the United States. His mother, Edna Lydington Towers, died in 2000. She was heir. . ." Anne couldn't make out anymore due to the bloodstains on the paper. She folded it back up and placed it in the old woman's raincoat pocket. "You came all this way to see me, and I couldn't help you."

As she waited for the police and Nigel, she examined the lantern. Why would a woman in the last minutes of her life hold a rusty old, 19th century iron lantern so dear? And, why didn't she want Anne to call the police? She didn't recognize the woman but the woman must have recognized Anne from the photo accompanying the article. She obviously was a fan. And, from the small smile she had given Anne when she opened the door, she had come to the Spoon Sisters' antique store, Great-Aunt Sybil's Attic, for a purpose. Of all the places she could have spent the last minutes of her life, she chose this tiny store in downtown suburban Glen Ellyn, Illinois.

Anne glanced over her shoulder at the portrait of Great-Aunt Sybil, where it had hung since the store had opened a few months ago. Anne always felt as if Aunt Sybil was watching over her through her portrait. Like the woman who now lay before Anne, Aunt Sybil had also come to a violent conclusion. Anne sat down next to the woman's body. She realized for the first time that she was shaking. She hugged herself and closed her eyes. She counted to ten. She could hear a voice inside her head—the voice of Great-Aunt Sybil. She opened her eyes and picked up the lantern. "Orphaned artifact," she said out loud.

Chapter Two

"Nick, you're bad. You're so bad," CC said with a giggle. Using her hip, she nudged Nick away from the stove. As much as she loved spicy food, even she would never put jalapenos in her chicken potpie. She had made the pie dough earlier from flour, butter and water. She'd simmered onions, carrots, potatoes and chicken in broth and cream until they were rich and thick. While her back was turned, Nick had added jalapeno pepper to kick up the spice. Like the potpie, her life had become spicier since she had met Nick. She watched as he chopped romaine lettuce, his muscles flexing with every stroke of the knife. She was amazed at how delicate his touch was in the kitchen and other rooms.

She popped the pies in the oven to bake. On the counter next to her, her phone pinged, alerting her to a text message. She washed her hands and picked up the iPhone. "CC, COME QUICK! I NEED YOU!" She read. CC sighed. She considered Anne's urgency on a sliding scale. It could range from winning an item on eBay to a great pending estate sale to an encounter with her on-again/off-again boyfriend, the very tall and very British police detective Nigel Towers. CC turned and looked at her current boyfriend, Nick. They had met through her cousin Ingrid and her boyfriend, another firefighter. *Where is Ingrid?* she thought. She'd been so wrapped up in dinner and Nick that she hadn't kept a close eye on her visiting much younger cousin. "Nick, have you heard from Adam or Ingrid? I haven't spoken to her all day," she said.

"Last I saw him was at the firehouse this afternoon. He didn't tell me where they were going," Nick said.

"Oh," CC said. She sent a quick text to her young cousin, asking where she was and when she'd be home. Then she sent another text to Anne, "What's up?" Nick wrapped his arms around her; she could smell the smoke and musk, the scent that he carried with him, the scent she had grown to love. He kissed her neck and then her phone pinged again.

CC looked at it to see a message from Ingrid. "At the store. Something horrible. Please come." She dialed Ingrid's number but it went straight to voicemail. She pulled the potpies out of the oven and turned it off. "Nick, we have to go to the store," she said. CC looked at the cooling potpies resting on top of the stove. Then she glanced at her Australian shepherd, Bandit, who was waiting with an intense stare in anticipation for them to leave so he could make quick work of the cooling pies. "Oh, no, you don't, Bandit," CC scolded. Bandit licked his chops and smiled. She put the potpies in the fridge.

"What's going on?" Nick asked.

"Trouble at the store. I can't make heads or tails of the text. Both Ingrid and Anne seem frantic." CC grabbed her raincoat. "We better go."

When they pulled up in front of the store, there was a line of police cars, an ambulance and fire truck, all lighting up the spring night. Nick ran over to one of the Glen Ellyn fire department EMTs. CC walked up the porch of the antique store. Anne was sitting in a 1920s burgundy cigar chair. Ingrid was sitting on its arm, holding Anne's hand as Anne spoke to the Glen Ellyn police detective. Detective Nigel Towers squatted on a child's stool, his spindly knees touching his chin. "What's going on here?" CC asked.

Anne looked up, not saying a word. "The Glen Ellyn police are handling it, CC," Nigel said.

"Handling what?" CC asked, looking at Anne.

Pulling out a lace handkerchief, Anne wiped a tear. "CC, one of our fans. She came for help. I couldn't help her. It was too late. She's dead."

CC glanced back at Nigel. "What is she talking about?"

"An old woman." He pulled a notebook out of his front jacket pocket. CC noticed he was wearing the paisley tie Anne had given him at Christmas. Every time Nigel was around Anne, he made sure to wear something she had given him no matter how outlandish it was. *It was rather endearing*, she thought. "She was carrying a forged Irish passport. They scanned her image into the Interpol system. Her name is Patricia Rounder. She's a British citizen," Nigel read from his notebook. "The car she was driving was stolen from long-term parking at O'Hare. That's all the Glen Ellyn police would tell me. She died from a stab wound."

"Stab wound? She was murdered?" CC asked. "What happened to her?"

Nigel had no answer.

"Anne, what was she doing here?" CC asked.

Anne shook her head. "I don't know. I closed up the shop and was getting ready to leave when she showed up."

"Adam's talking with the paramedics. He'll find out more," Ingrid said. CC still had mixed emotions about her cousin dating a young fireman. He was nice enough but she felt protective of the girl even though she had no such qualms about dating a fireman herself.

Nigel interrupted, "I'll have a word with the Glen Ellyn police."

"Thank you. Thank you, all." Anne said, gazing around at her friends. "Ingrid, do you think you could go in back and make me a cup of tea?"

"Certainly, Anne."

"Nigel, CC?" Ingrid asked.

CC nodded.

"No tea for me," Nigel said.

As Ingrid walked away, CC watched the young police officers and paramedics stop to turn and watch the girl. CC sighed. Her beautiful young cousin had that effect on men. CC constantly worried about her. Nick and Adam came into the store and knelt down next to Anne. "Anne, there's nothing you could have done," Nick said. "Frankie—that's the paramedic. He's from our firehouse. He said she lost too much blood even before she got here."

Anne felt the dampness on her Capri pant leg. Glancing down, she saw for the first time she was covered in blood. "She wasn't making any sense. She seemed very confused," Anne said.

"She was in shock. You couldn't have saved her," Nigel said.

Ingrid's handsome young fireman Adam took Anne's hand in his. "Nick and I are heading to the bar. Why don't you all come over when you're done and have a drink?"

Anne nodded.

Nick glanced at CC and gave her a crooked smile. Adam left the store. "Anne, do you want me to stay with you?" Nigel asked.

"No, Nigel, now that CC's here, I'll be fine," Anne said. "Thank you for coming out and for everything."

Nigel's knees creaked as he hopped off the stool with his grasshopper legs. He leaned over and kissed Anne on the forehead. "Annie, if you want to talk later, call me. I'm on duty but I'm always a phone call away."

"Thank you, Nigel." Anne gave him a kiss on his cheek and then he was gone.

CC pulled a chair up next to Anne. She took Anne's hands in hers.

Ingrid walked in, carrying a silver tray and tea service. Anne glanced at it. "I was hoping you would use the Rogers set." She peeked around the tray. "No cookies?"

"I could go look. There might be some in the pantry," Ingrid said, setting the tray down on a damask-covered pouf.

CC grabbed Ingrid's hand and shook her head.

"Don't bother," Anne said. "I looked earlier."

"I thought you were on your low carb diet," CC said.

"No, I'm doing the Whole 30."

"What's that?"

Anne perked up. "Whole 30 is a way of ridding your body of all impurities and chemicals. You eat very specific foods for 30 days. It's supposed to help you get rid of your cravings while restarting your metabolism. You eat meat, fish, vegetables, some fruit and eliminate all processed food, sugar, dairy and alcohol."

"Like cookies?" CC asked.

"How's it working for you?" Ingrid asked.

"I've gained two pounds," Anne said.

Glen Ellyn police detective Rick Phillips came up to them. "Miss Hillstrom, we're finished here. We'll have some more questions later, I'm sure."

"Did she have any family?" Anne asked.

"As of yet, we haven't found any next of kin," the detective replied.

"She's not from Glen Ellyn. Nigel said she was carrying a forged Irish passport."

"We're contacting the embassy," the detective said.

"Oh, dear," Anne said. "So far from home. No one to mourn her. No one to care." Anne's eyes teared up. Ingrid put her arm around her.

"Miss Hillstrom, we'll let you know what we find out," Detective Phillips said before leaving the store. After all the first responders had gone, CC locked the door behind them. "What did Patricia say to you?"

Anne sipped her tea. "She begged me to open the door. When she came in, she collapsed. I brought her some water."

"She didn't say a word to you?"

"She handed me the lantern and then she died."

"Lantern?"

"Oh, yes, I forgot to tell the police. She was carrying this lantern." Anne ran to the counter and reached underneath it to one of the shelves. "It's nothing very special." Anne held up the black cast iron lantern, its bottom encased in elaborate scrollwork. "It appears to be late 1800s. I thought she came to sell it. She was wearing a pretty shabby secondhand raincoat. Maybe something you'd find at Savers or Goodwill. I would have bought it from her. I would have helped."

"I know, Anne, I know you would." CC took the lantern from Anne, studied it for a moment before setting it down, putting her arms around her friend and hugging her. "Let's go home. You've had quite an ordeal."

"Nick and Adam want us to come to the bar. Aren't we going?" Anne asked.

"Ingrid has school tomorrow, and you should rest. I have some pot pies I can heat up."

Anne thought about her Whole 30 that she'd been on for a whole two days. Bread was off limits. Potpie sounded tempting, too tempting to refuse. "You're right. Let's go home." She finished her tea and grabbed her navy 1940s Aquarock raincoat from the oak hall tree by the front door. CC and Ingrid grabbed umbrellas from the majolica umbrella stand in the corner. The two walked outside. The torrential rain was pouring sideways, the sky lit up by lightning. Anne reached for an umbrella and stared at the umbrella stand—the one that was gifted to her by her Great-Aunt Sybil, the one that she had bought back from Betsy Buttersworth. "Buttersworth," she muttered. The lightning struck, illuminating Great-Aunt Sybil's portrait. Anne smiled at her aunt. She grabbed the lantern, flew out the door and locked it behind her.

Chapter Three

"Dear Friends," CC typed after opening up her Spoon Sisters blog in which she and Anne chronicled their antique hunting adventures. "I apologize but the store will be closed tomorrow. I wanted to let you know in case you were planning a visit. Anne had quite the scare last night. One of our fans stopped by the store after hours and the unthinkable happened." CC paused. *How much to share*, she pondered. "I can't share the details right now but, as the story unravels, I'll be sure to share more.

"Ingrid has been settling in well. Even though she is busy with classes at Columbia, she still finds time to help us at Great-Aunt Sybil's Attic. She has made some lovely finds on her own, including this Persian rug, a steal at Goodwill for $5.99, and antique flatware, $1 each at an estate sale." CC posted pictures of the items to the blog. She heard a thump from upstairs and sighed. She loved her dear friend, Anne, but friends don't always make the best houseguests. She grabbed Bandit's leash. "Come on, Boo, let's go for a walk." They headed out the door.

Anne rolled over in bed, reaching over the side for her phone. She was watching a Limoges plate on eBay. After increasing her bid, she rolled back and threw the covers over her head. She had not slept well. She kicked the blankets and sat up on the edge of the bed. She heard a screech in the hallway. She navigated around the boxes and suitcases that were piled haphazardly on the floor. She stuck her head out the door to see her white Persian Sassy and her kitten, Sybil, chasing Bandit down the hallway. This was not the usual posturing for an Australian shepherd but Sassy and Sybil would have none of his bullying. They had taken over CC's house just as Anne had. She stepped around the suitcases that were creeping into the hallway. What little furniture she had rescued from the fire that had destroyed her own house was now part of CC's. It had been five months since that tragedy. She hurriedly closed the bedroom door so CC couldn't see the clutter. As she pushed the door shut, there was a tap. Ingrid popped her head in. "Anne, CC wanted me to get you for breakfast." Ingrid scanned the room and smiled.

"I'll be right down," Anne said. Anne stood in front of the full-length mirror admiring her vintage Japanese silk kimono. It was a gift from Nigel. She imagined an American soldier buying it for his bride back home. She twisted left and right and then turned her back to the mirror, looking over her shoulder. She had lost a lot of weight since Christmas. She scoured the clothes scattered on the dresser, chair and floor. She hoped that her flowered Capri pants would fit. They had gotten a little less snug since she'd started her new diet. She pulled them on and tugged on the zipper. Perfect. She grabbed a cotton crop top. Perhaps a little too young for a woman fortyish but she thought she could pull it off. She headed downstairs. She could smell CC's egg soufflé. It was thoughtful of her friend not to tempt her to stray from her Whole 30 diet. She had switched from low carb to Whole 30 so she could indulge in a late night dream-fueled snack of Brie and grapes.

Ingrid was making coffee in CC's French press. "That smells great, CC," Anne said, plopping down in a kitchen chair. Like the rest of CC's house, it was immaculate—too immaculate—if you asked Anne. The house needed to look lived in, feel lived in.

Ingrid brought Anne a cup of coffee. Anne reached for the sugar cubes. CC snapped her head around as if she knew what was about to happen. Anne pulled her hand back and sipped her coffee. "So, Ingrid, how's school going?"

"Very good, Anne, I am working on story structure for my creative writing class. Structure, plotting, characterization, call to action," Ingrid said.

"What's the theme?"

"We have to write about a hero."

"Oh really?" Anne sipped her coffee, grimacing at the bitter taste. Surely, one sugar cube wouldn't hurt. Sassy jumped up on the table and leapt onto the china cabinet followed by Sybil. They both sat patiently waiting for the food to be brought to Anne, who they knew would share with them. Anne could sense their Cheshire grins beneath their placid expressions. Sybil had become quite the troublemaker. Not quite eight months old, she had already followed in her mother's paw steps—stealing bits of twine, knocking over boxes, always looking for treasure.

"I want to pick somebody I know. Perhaps not a traditional historical figure but a real-life figure," Ingrid said.

CC grinned as she flipped the bacon. What better hero for her cousin than herself, an established journalist, a real writer. As she turned around to accept the honor, Ingrid said, "You, Anne. I want to write about you."

Anne beamed, grabbing Ingrid's hands. "Oh, that's just fabulous. What a story. It's like the phoenix rising out of the ashes."

"I've read every one of your blogs."

CC frowned, thinking *her* blogs?

"Anne, you've taught me so much about antique hunting," Ingrid continued.

CC turned back to the bacon and lined the pieces in an orderly row on a paper towel.

"Ingrid, what do you say I take you out for lunch later, and we can get started?" Anne said.

"Danke," Ingrid said.

"Bitte," Anne replied.

"Oh, Anne, your German is getting much better."

CC grimaced. "Speaking of German, have you spoken with your mother lately?"

"I texted her."

"No, have you spoken to her, on the phone? I think you should let her know how school is going. And have you told her about Adam?"

"Yes, cousin CC, she knows about Adam, and she approves."

"You should call your mother," Anne whispered. "CC feels responsible for you. Being a stranger in a strange country."

CC took the egg soufflés out of the oven. She placed the hot tray on her Danish modern table. After it cooled, she sliced squares and placed one on a plate for each of them. Anne took a big whiff. "It smells delicious, CC," Anne said. She took the fatty part of a piece of bacon and reached it over her head to the shelf. Sybil nibbled it away. Another piece followed for Sassy.

"Don't encourage them, Anne," CC scolded. "Have you heard anything from the Glen Ellyn police about Ms. Rounder?"

"Nigel texted me this morning that the stolen car in front of the store had her fingerprints all over it. There was blood all over the seat. The police are trying to locate her next of kin now."

"What a terrible night," CC said.

"Yes, it was terrible." Anne shivered, recalling all the blood. "I'm meeting Nigel for dinner tonight. I'm sure he'll know more by then."

"And, how are the plans for the new house going?" CC asked, moving a stack of Anne's mail to the side of the table.

"I'm glad you asked." Anne reached down into her large orange Prada bag. "I've got some swatches for the sofa." She pulled out fabric swatches followed by tile samples. "And some tile samples for the *en suite* master bathroom."

"You haven't even broke ground yet," CC said.

"I know it's taking a little longer than we thought to get the permit approved, and I've had to make small adjustments to the plans."

"What kind of adjustments?"

"Well, the lot is only 65 feet wide so we have to build vertical for the square footage I want, but the city has height restrictions. I guess because of low-flying planes out of O'Hare."

CC laughed. "How high are you planning on going?"

"Maybe four or five stories."

CC smiled, cradling her coffee mug.

"The architect is stopping by this morning."

They finished their breakfast. The doorbell rang. Bandit took off toward the front door, barking. Sassy and Sybil hid behind one of Anne's moving boxes that filled the living room. "That must be Terrence now." Anne rushed to the door. A handsome young man in khakis and a crisp white cotton shirt, holding a laptop, waited for her on the porch. "Oh, Terrence, come in."

Ingrid and CC watched as Anne cleared the catalogs, mail and brochures from the dining room table creating a pile on the floor. "Hi, Terrence. Anne, we're going to get going—Ingrid and I—to open the store," CC said.

Terrence nodded a hello before opening his laptop and setting it on the table.

After they left and Anne handed him a coffee mug, he pulled up a rendering on his computer. "I've made the modifications that you requested," he said.

Anne studied them.

"The city ordinance won't allow us to go over four stories unless it's a commercial development and your lot is not zoned commercial," Terrence said.

Anne continued to ponder the rendering. "Bigger. I want bigger." Anne stretched her arms out wide. "The staircase has to be marble and grand. I always dreamed of swooshing down a marble staircase in a ball gown. Now the question is: imported Italian marble or domestic?"

The frazzled young man shook his head. "Miss Hillstrom, you're talking about at least a ten percent increase in your budget for a marble entryway, and if you're talking about imported Italian marble, add another eight percent above that."

"Yes, but this is what I want." Anne pulled out her iPhone. "I want my staircase to look like this." She pulled up pictures of Chicago's Driehaus Museum, the restored Gilded Age mansion. Its curving staircase wound around on two sides sculptured out of Italian marble with African mahogany railings. Anne had called to see if the museum was for sale. It was not. "Think Xanadu."

The young architect blinked.

"You know *Citizen Kane*, the movie? The Winchester House? San Simeon? The Biltmore? Any of these ring a bell? You are an architect, aren't you?"

"Miss Hillstrom, you're way over your budget."

"Did you see me blink? I'll worry about the money. You worry about the Italian imported marble." Anne paused. "No, wait, I'll worry about the marble. I think I might need to go hand pick it." Visions of Italy danced in her head. She could smell the Tuscan bread slathered with olive oil and garlic baked in wood-fired ovens. The steaming bowls of pappa al pomodoro, fresh bread, tomato soup. It had been a year since she'd had real authentic French food so the thought of sipping wine at an Italian vineyard was almost as intoxicating as hand picking her Carrara marble. As she drifted off, the young architect gathered up his notes.

"Miss Hillstrom, Miss Hillstrom."

"Call me Anne," she said, snapping out of her Italian food-induced reverie.

"Anne, I'll make the changes and give you the new budget."

"Well, thank you, Terrence. I hope you get it right this time." Anne waved her hand. "Thank you, Terrence."

With that, Terrence was gone. Anne sat down at the dining room table, perusing the blueprints. Catalogs of luxury homes surrounded her as did samples of fabrics, tile and other fixtures. Her plans for the new house had quickly become a full-time job beside the other hats she wore. Anne Hillstrom, antique hunter, chemist, entrepreneur and business owner. "Hat rack. I saw an antique brass one." She flipped on her iPhone and scanned her eBay watch list, scrolling down the first 300 items, until she came to the antique Victorian brass hat rack. From under the paisley fabric on the floor, a little white fluffy head popped out. The little white Persian pounced. "Sybil, what are you up to?" Anne asked.

Sybil stared up at Anne, blinking her one blue and one green eye. "Where's your momma?" Anne asked. Sybil climbed up Anne's leg then sat on her lap purring, while Anne petted her soft fur, thumbing through her eBay watch list. "Not quite what I'm looking for." Anne set her phone down.

Her new house would never replace her home. That would take time. The fire had destroyed brick and mortar but not the memories she had made there. Those she carried with her. She whispered into Sybil's ear, "Life is about acquiring memories. In the end, that's all we have."

Chapter Four

"I don't know how much more of this I can take, Ingrid," CC said as she unlocked the front door of Great-Aunt Sybil's Attic. CC loved that first whiff of must and memories that assaulted her each time she opened the door. She and Anne had managed to find a wonderful collection of vintage clothing, antique furniture, salvaged yard art. Their dream of building a business out of their antiquing hobby was now a reality. Their blog fan list had doubled and, for the first time in a long time, CC was in a healthy relationship with a very healthy fireman.

"What do you mean, CC?" Ingrid asked, turning on the lights in the store.

CC flipped the closed sign to *open* in the front window. "It's too much. There's too much everything. Boxes, clothes, ribbons and bows. Wait, I sound like a Dr. Seuss book, but it's true. It's like having *Thing Number 1* and *Thing Number 2* living in my house."

"I love having Aunt Anne live with us," Ingrid said.

"Aunt Anne?" CC asked.

"She told me to call her Aunt Anne."

"I love her. She's my dearest friend but she's got to go," CC said.

"It's not forever. She is building a house."

"She's not building a house, she's building a mansion. And, like the Winchester House, I have a feeling it will never be finished."

"Oh, Cousin CC, you are funny."

"No, I mean it. Anne is caught up in all the majesty of it. None of her plans are practical. Her electrical bills alone will be outrageous. She needs a reality check." CC paused for a moment. "Never mind, let's get ready to open. I have a hundred texts and emails from fans who are coming today for our vintage linen trunk show."

"Cousin CC, I want to thank you again. This has been a dream being able to work at the Spoon Sisters antique store, staying with you, going to school."

CC gave Ingrid a hug. "I love having you here. Never mind me; I'm a little crabby. I didn't get much sleep last night."

"I know. I heard you come in. It must have been after three. What were you doing up so late?"

"Never mind," CC said.

The door opened, jingling the silver bell that hung from the transom. It signaled their workday had begun. Several customers filed in. One of them CC recognized. "Abby," CC greeted her.

"Oh, CC, the store looks wonderful," Abby said.

"Thank you," CC said, turning to Ingrid. "This is Abby Roberts. She was one of our original Spoon Sisters blog fans. Well, back then it was called *From the Estate* but after we solved the estate sale murders," she paused, "well, you know the whole story, it became the Spoon Sisters blog."

"CC, I was so excited when I read about your trunk sale. I'm planning a wedding, and the bride wants vintage Irish linens for the tables," Abby said.

"Ingrid, Abby's a wedding planner, by the way."

"How fun," Ingrid said before moving away to ring up a sale.

"Anne will be sorry she missed you," CC said to Abby. "She's been scouring estate sales for these linens. Come over here; I put them to the side for you."

CC didn't tell her that she'd been holding them *from* Anne. "How large is the wedding?"

"Three hundred guests. It's at the Sanfilippo estate in Barrington."

"That's amazing. How'd you manage that?" CC asked.

"The bride is a distant relative of the Sanfilippo family, and she's making it a charitable event by asking guests to donate to the Field Museum."

"She must know the Field Museum's curator Wayne Muscarello," CC said. "Anne and I are quite good friends with Wayne. Anne's Great-Aunt Sybil donated her Viking sword collection to the Field."

"I'll have to ask her," Abby said.

"What's so special about the estate?" Ingrid asked.

CC turned to Ingrid. "I've never been to the estate but I've read a lot about it. You know, Ingrid, the estate is known for having the largest collection of automatic musical instruments. Its Wurlitzer pipe organ has almost 5,000 pipes. It also has a steam locomotive and a beautiful carousel." She turned back to Abby. "Come see what I have for you. We don't quite have enough for 300 guests but we have a good start." CC pulled out a large container and opened its lid.

Abby sifted through the linens, sorting them by color and size. "I think these are perfect." She stopped for a moment, gazing around the store. "We're also looking for flower vases. The bride would like antique crystal so it sparkles in the candlelight."

"I have a whole cabinet of Waterford crystal vases from the early 1900s. I also have some Lalique and Orrefors. How about napkin rings?" CC asked.

"I have some pretty rings but I don't think they'll go with the Waterford or Irish linen. We might need you to find some napkin rings as well. It doesn't have to be matchy match—that's part of the charm of this wedding. The bride wants each table to be unique."

"You know, Abby, if you're looking at thirty tables between the Irish linen, the Waterford, the napkin rings, that's quite a lot of money for one day especially if the proceeds are for charity. I hate to see you spend a lot of money on decorations," CC said.

"What'd you have in mind?"

"I'd have to talk to Anne but I don't think there'd be much of a problem. Perhaps we could rent everything to you for the day. In fact, Anne and I would be happy to come out, deliver the materials and decorate the tables."

"Really?" Abby asked.

"When is the wedding?"

"August 12."

"Let me come up with some numbers and talk to Anne. I think it'd be fun. Anne's always wanted to see the mansion," CC said with a forced smile and then she glanced at Ingrid who was helping a young couple who were looking at a dining room set Anne had found at an estate sale. It was rosewood with rectangular scrolled edges and bear claw legs. "Here, sit on the chairs. We reupholstered it because the original upholstery was in bad shape. The wood is original. We only used Murphy's soap to bring out the luster."

The woman sat on the chair. "It's very comfortable and solid." She ran her hand along the tabletop.

"All the legs are glued and screwed with dovetailed joints. All solid wood, no veneer, no particleboard. We have the matching breakfront and buffet, if you are interested." Ingrid pointed to the two larger pieces.

The woman took out her iPhone. "Ingrid, would you mind I took a selfie with you?"

"With me, really?" Ingrid cracked a large smile.

"I have to admit I'm a bit of a fan. When I read about your adventures with Anne and CC, I had to come meet you in person."

"Really?"

"I have to confess. I'm here for more than a dining room set even though I do love it."

"How can I help you?" Ingrid sat down on the chair across from her.

"My aunt passed away recently."

"I'm so sorry." Ingrid paused.

"Kimberly," the woman interjected. "Thank you. When we were clearing out her house, we found her collection of Hummels. Actually, it's more than a collection. It has to be at least several hundred."

"Oh, I love Hummels."

"Some of them she brought with her from Germany."

"Oh, you're German. That's wonderful," Ingrid said.

"Yes, that was part of the reason I wanted to meet you. I read that you were from Germany and that you were staying here with CC. I thought maybe my cousin would be a little more open to dealing with you because you're German."

"I would love to see the Hummels and meet your cousin. My grandmother collected Hummels. She's from Munich. I have a couple of hers. I'm very familiar with them. Let me talk to my bosses and maybe we can come out to the house and look around. Are you working with an estate sale company?" Ingrid asked.

"No, my cousin, Gertrude, the executor, hasn't hired a company yet."

"I'll talk to Anne and CC, and if you okay it with Gertrude, we'll come out and maybe we can look at more than the Hummels."

"That would be wonderful. I'll call you and let you know after I talk to Gertrude. I have to warn you. She can be difficult to deal with."

"What about the dining room set?" Ingrid asked.

"I love it. Do you deliver?"

Ingrid thought for a moment. "Actually, I could talk to my boyfriend. He has a pick-up truck."

"That would be great. Here's my number." Kimberly handed her a card.

Ingrid walked Kimberly to the cash register.

That afternoon after the last customer left, CC and Ingrid walked out onto the sidewalk. CC turned to lock the front door and noticed there were lights on in the shop next door, the former sweet shop. It had been boarded up for a while. She hoped someone was restoring it. Depending on the business, it could add to the charm of the quaint downtown and attract more customers. But another sweet shop might be too much for Anne to endure.

They climbed into CC's lime green-and-white 1968 VW bus. CC had lovingly restored it, bolt by bolt, after finding it buried in a Southern Illinois barn. They drove down Main Street, Ingrid's face lit up by the glow of her iPhone. CC thought how teenagers were the same no matter where they were from. She looked sideways at Ingrid. She'd be nineteen in a few months and even though CC didn't think it was possible, she was becoming more beautiful. She hoped that she was a good mentor and a good friend to her young cousin. Ingrid and Anne had instantly bonded and seemed more like family than CC and Ingrid. It was a passing thought.

She turned down Pennsylvania Avenue and pulled in front of Nick's Bar—her boyfriend's bar. The 19th century fire hose wagon they'd found stood in front, underneath the red awning. She could see through the window Adam and Nick shooting pool. In another hour, the bar would be crowded with firemen from the first shift, but for now, Nick had time for her. She followed Ingrid inside. "Hi, Nick, Adam," CC said.

They put their pool sticks down and came over. Nick hugged CC while Adam hugged Ingrid. CC still couldn't get used to the ripples in Nick's muscled back as he hugged her. His strong arms wrapped around her. "Have you guys eaten?" Nick asked.

"No, we locked up the shop. I could do with a bite," CC said.

Adam went back behind the bar to pull some beers for the firemen who were walking in. Ingrid followed him.

"CC, come back in the kitchen." Nick held the swinging kitchen door open for her. She slid past him into the small galley kitchen. As the door swung closed, Nick grabbed her by the arm, turned her around and kissed her on the lips. Then he kissed her again.

CC lost all thought of food. Regretfully she pulled back and cleared her throat. "Nick, we stopped by to see if you'd heard anything more about Patricia Rounder. I can't stay long; Ingrid shouldn't be in here."

"Sit down. Let me get you a glass of wine or something." Nick poured two glasses of his homemade wine. He handed one to CC and sat across from her. "I talked with Detective Phillips; we're on the same basketball league. They tore apart the stolen car that Patricia Rounder was driving, and they found blood on the tire iron. It wasn't her blood."

"Really? That's interesting."

"That's all they know right now."

"I appreciate it." CC finished her wine. She walked over to the stove, lifted the lid on the stockpot. She took a big whiff, smelling the full bold richness of Guinness. "Irish stew."

"Beef short ribs. I like to slow cook them with onions and beer." Nick stood behind her, pressing up against her back.

"Wish I could stay. It smells great but I want to get Ingrid home."

"I'll deliver some later tonight." Nick smiled again.

CC smiled. She was hungry again but this time not for food.

Chapter Five

Anne wandered back to her seat, carrying her third plate of crab legs with a generous side of drawn butter. She sat down across from Nigel. He had brought her to Shaw's Crabhouse for their Saturday night all-you-can-eat crab buffet. Anne snapped the king crab leg open while Nigel struggled with his crab cracker. His long, bony fingers wrapped around the tiny cracker. Anne continued to snap the legs using her hands with the precision of a sea otter. She soaked up the butter, not saying a word in her seafood-eating frenzy. Nigel smiled as he attempted to crack one leg open. Anne reached over and snapped it with her hands for him.

"I love this place, Nigel; great suggestion." Anne said, downing her third Mai Tai. She was comfortably full but not full enough to stop. She continued her assault.

Nigel continued, "Anne, you must tell me about the plans for your new house. How are they coming?"

"Oh, Nigel, let me show you." After wiping her hands on her napkin, she reached into her large orange Prada bag and pulled out her iPad mini. She brought up the latest renderings that resembled a medieval castle complete with turrets and a watchtower. She flipped the pad around and placed it on the table in front of Nigel.

Nigel laughed. "No, really, Anne, seriously. How are the plans going?"

"What do you mean? Those are the plans."

Nigel studied the drawing. "It looks like Downton Abbey."

"That's my favorite show."

"But Anne. How will that fit into your neighborhood? Onto your lot? What will the neighbors say?"

"It's not going to be as big as Downton Abbey, silly goose," Anne said. "I'm going to expand my lot. I've been talking to my neighbors on the south about buying their house. Then I'll tear it down and build on a double lot."

Nigel's concern grew. "Anne, how much will this cost?"

Anne licked the butter off her fingers. "The numbers aren't all in yet. I'm still waiting on an estimate for my marble buying trip to Italy and the custom copper sinks and faucets. There are just so many details. It's exhausting."

Nigel wiped the butter off his chin. Anne glanced at him as Nigel noticed the little piece of crab in his moustache. Well, not really a moustache. More of a good old English try at a moustache. Nigel had taken to growing different stages of facial hair over the last year. For a while, it was a bit of a scraggly beard, then the goatee—not a good look for a man with such a thin face. Now the moustache. Anne thought at times that Nigel resembled Ichabod Crane come to life—very tall, very skinny. Or at least the Disney cartoon version. His eyes sparkled and his smile lit up the room. He tried very hard to hide his British accent, not that he was embarrassed by his Cockney lilt, more that he loved America and all things American. Whether it was gangster-filled film noir movies, big band dancing, classic muscle cars or even pop songs. "Nigel," Anne said.

"Yes, Annie?"

"Have you ever been to Italy? Specifically the Tuscany area?"

"No, Annie, I have not."

"Oh, you think that's someplace you'd like to go sometime?"

"I think that would be aces."

"I'm thinking about a buying trip there to pick out my Carrara marble. Oh," Anne said as the waiter brought over a dessert sampler filled with mini raspberry pies, key lime tarts and carrot cake. Anne's attention drifted to the sweet temptations. Which one to start with? Was it best to start tart and then move to sweet cream cheese frosting? Or the other way around? It was a continuum of delicious choices.

"Anne, are you serious about going to Italy to pick out marble for your abbey?" Nigel asked, interrupting her thoughts.

She held one whipped cream covered spoon up in the air. "Nigel, it's not an abbey. I've got another name picked out. And, I'm still waiting for all the numbers to come in. I'm having some troubles with my people." Anne became irritated. *Why was everyone so focused on her house and its cost?*

"It seems very nice but very expensive. When does construction begin?"

"We're still waiting on the permits but the city says they won't grant them until I finalize the plans. I've been through several change orders just on the design alone. But at least I've ordered fixtures, fabric, flooring."

"Without finalizing the exact dimensions?" Nigel asked.

"I had to act quickly. There was a demolition sale on the Internet for old hand-scraped flooring from an 18th century manor in Belgium. I didn't want to lose it." Anne didn't mention the French oak fireplace surround or the travertine tile from a villa in Italy.

"When is it being delivered? And, what are you going to do with it?"

"It clears customs next week. I'm going to rent a storage locker for it until we're ready." Anne failed to mention her other five storage lockers that had been accumulating treasures since she'd collected her reward money.

"I think it will be lovely. A fitting castle for a queen."

Anne smiled, picturing the tiara she was watching on eBay. While Nigel continued eating, she glanced down at her lap where she had her iPhone open to her eBay watch list. The tiara was up to $9,000, almost the same price of the Viking stove that she planned to order. She might, mind you, *might* have to start making difficult choices, but not yet. She clicked bid. She looked up at Nigel with a smile and a little bit of raspberry filling clinging to the corner of her mouth. Nigel fought the urge to reach over and dab it off for her.

There was so much he wanted to do for her and so little he wouldn't do for her. He fought so many urges when it came to Anne but he held himself back because it had been his idea to let the kettle steep He needed to take things slow and build on their friendship to see if love would grow. For Nigel, that seed was planted the day Anne Hillstrom had shown up at his police station. That seed had flowered into love for the woman sitting across from him. Even if it meant living in Hillstrom Manor. He wondered if she'd make him wear dinner jackets and tails. Not a good look for a man of his build.

The waiter brought over the check. Nigel reached for it but Anne held out her hand and grabbed it first. "No, Anne, I insist," he said. "You're my guest."

"No, Nigel, let me take care of this," she argued half-heartedly.

"Anne, I wouldn't feel right. You have to save your money for Italy and the new house." Nigel grabbed the check from Anne's hand, running his finger against her wrist. He paid the bill and walked Anne out to her 1992 Mercury Mystique, which was overflowing with the day's spoils from her busy day of shopping, or *work* as she preferred to call it. Nigel bent over and peeked inside. Barely enough room for the driver. All the other seats were occupied with Anne's passengers which included picture frames, antique hatboxes, an ornate wrought iron doorstop and a collection of cigar boxes. "Annie, have you thought about a new car?"

"Oh, no, why would I need a new car?" She reached in her purse for her keys and papers flew out onto the ground.

Nigel reached down and picked them up, handing them to her. "I'm saying it would be more practical and probably safer to buy a new car."

"Oh, no, that's not very fun. Besides these old cars have so much interior room and big trunks."

After seeing the interior, Nigel wondered what was in the trunk. "I've had a very nice evening." Nigel stood awkwardly, hovering over Anne deciding whether to kiss her, hug her or say goodbye. As he started the long journey down to kiss her cheek, his phone rang. He reached in his suit jacket pocket. "Yes, this is Detective Towers. Oh, I see." He listened for a few moments. "Thank you, sergeant. I appreciate the update. Yes, please do keep me informed." Nigel hung up. "Anne, that was the Glen Ellyn police. The woman who died in your store, Patricia Rounder, was a fugitive. She was wanted by the Gardai."

"What's that?"

"Gardai is the Irish police."

"What was she wanted for?" Anne asked.

"For murder."

Chapter Six

Anne drove down Interstate 355, the word *murder* echoing in her head. She pictured Patricia Rounder and saw red, the same color of the three Mai Tais she'd just downed, which were now losing their effect, leaving a headache behind. Her mind drifted back to that night and the lantern, which now lay in her trunk. Lay. *Laid to rest*, she thought. *Poor Patricia*.

She didn't notice the tollbooth until it was too late. She slammed on her brakes, her foot touching the floor. Her brakes squealed and cried out in pain. The 1992 Mercury Mystique fishtailed, barely missing the Illinois State trooper who was parked alongside the tollbooth building. She finally stopped when she slammed into a 55-gallon drum which exploded with sand from the impact. Anne's heart was beating rapidly, her hands locked onto the wheel. All she could think about was Nigel warning her about her car. Her faulty brakes, no airbags, her dashboard now filled with Nordstrom Rack bags that had tumbled forward. Her large orange Prada bag had flipped over on the floor, spilling out her collection of thimbles, perfume bottles and unopened bills. She threw the car into park, and sat staring ahead, trying to calm her breathing by counting to ten. The tap on the driver's window startled her. The trooper motioned for her to open her window. Anne cranked the window down.

"Ma'am, are you all right?" he asked with a concerned look.

Anne looked around at the devastation in the car. She had heard crystal crashing, a sound that shattered her heart. "No, I'm certainly not all right."

"Do you need medical attention?" The trooper stuck his head in the window and took a deep breath. "Ma'am have you been drinking?"

"No, well, I mean to say, I came from dinner. I had a drink with dinner."

"Ma'am, I'm going to need you to step out of your vehicle, please."

Still shaking, Anne opened the driver's door with a creak and stepped into the cold late spring air. The trooper walked her over to the shoulder of the road. "Ma'am, I need to see your driver's license, proof of insurance and registration."

Anne thought about her glove compartment and everything that was crammed in it. It had burst open on impact and its contents were now scattered on the passenger floor. She started to cry. The young trooper took her by the arm and sat her on a bench under a light in front of the maintenance building. He spoke into his shoulder two-way radio. Minutes later, an ambulance pulled up. The paramedics checked Anne over, taking her blood pressure. "Are you in any pain?"

"No, really, I'm fine. My brakes gave out. I had them checked not too long ago but they were fine. They just went out. I couldn't stop."

The paramedics walked away with the trooper. They spoke for a few minutes and came back to Anne. "Miss Hillstrom, I need you to take a breathalyzer test," the trooper said.

"That's crazy; I didn't drink that much. It was just one mai tai." Anne didn't think to tell him about the second one or the third one. "I told you it was my brakes. They went out."

"We have a tow truck coming for your car. I need to test your blood-alcohol level." He held out a little tester.

Anne blew into the tester. She was under the legal limit, but just barely. "Excuse me, Miss Hillstrom." The trooper went back to his cruiser, sat in the driver's seat and clicked on his computer. He read the long list of parking violations, her failed emissions test, her driving without registration. He came back over with several yellow envelopes and handed them to her.

"What are these?" Anne stared at the envelopes.

"Ma'am, you have several outstanding driving violations. You're going to need someone to pick you up. You'll have to go to court to get your license back and to clear up all these tickets. Do you want me to call someone for you?"

Anne sighed. She didn't want to call CC but CC was her *ICE*—in case of emergency. She had used that card too many times in the past so she called Ingrid. "Ingrid, it's Anne. Listen carefully; is CC home?"

"Yes, she's asleep."

"Good. I need you to grab her keys and come get me," Anne explained where she was. As she waited for Ingrid, she watched her Mercury Mystique, more dented than not, being dragged away by the Lincoln towing truck. "Wait!" she screamed after it and ran toward the tow truck. "I have to get my stuff out."

Stopping the truck, the driver hopped out of the cab and peeked inside the car that was filled to the dome light with bags, boxes and baubles. Anne reached inside and grabbed what she could. She shoved things into her large orange Prada bag. Then the tow truck took off, leaving Anne behind. All Anne could hear was her bumper scraping along the road and the word *murder* echoing in her head.

Chapter Seven

"Have you seen Anne?" CC asked Ingrid as she unlocked the door to the antique store.

"Not this morning." Ingrid shook her head, keeping her promise to not divulge Anne's accident to her cousin.

CC pulled out the wrought iron yard art and furniture they had found at a recent estate sale. With summer on its way, many customers were looking for lawn ornaments, patio furniture and planters. She arranged them on the front porch, making a cozy seating arrangement. Ingrid adjusted the large Oriental planters by the front door.

They heard a honking of a horn from down the block. Bright LED headlights pierced through the morning mist. A metallic gold Mercedes G-class SUV, the size of a small tank, rumbled down the street, headed toward CC and Ingrid. Its driver landed the yacht in front of the store, waving her arm through the window and honking loudly. "Come and take a look at my new car," Anne called.

CC glanced at Anne then at Ingrid then at Anne again. "Ohmigosh," she said.

Anne climbed down out of the truck. "Look at the room in the back. I won't need to call you anymore, CC, when I find furniture or large antiques."

CC stood, shaking her head, with her mouth open, unable to speak.

"I got all the bells and whistles—Napa leather seats, sunroof, GPS system, 18-speaker Bose sound system.

Oh, and it's real wood trim on the dashboard." Anne waved her arms around, enthusing over the features as though she was a model in a car showroom.

"This is great, Anne." Ingrid climbed into the driver's seat and put her hands on the steering wheel. "Can I borrow it sometime?"

"Sure," Anne said. "This is the best part. Look at the navigation system. It has 80-gigabyte memory. I can program all estate sales and auction houses and flea markets. It practically drives itself."

CC walked over and glanced at the window sticker. The first line that jumped out at her was $119,000. "Anne, ohmigosh, $119,000," she said, reading the sticker.

"Don't be silly. That's the asking price. I had them knock off $2,000."

"Anne, are you serious? How can you ever afford this? The payments must be outrageous."

"Don't be silly," Anne repeated. "I paid cash. My reward money. It was time I got a new car."

Ingrid exchanged a knowing glance with Anne. CC sighed. "Anne, we had this talk after you received the award money. You promised me that you were going to invest and not spend it all."

"This is an investment. I can use it to find items for the store. It's tax deductible. It's a legitimate business expense."

CC couldn't argue with her logic. "What about your house? I saw your plans. You're way over budget."

"I've been thinking about the house plans, and I realized in all the excitement I was kind of going overboard so I'm going to change it to an English craftsman style. I decided I don't need Downton Abbey. I'd be just as happy in a smaller, cozier home. I'm keeping the library and the greenhouse and the gazebo but this is much more practical for my neighborhood and for my lifestyle. I already called Terrence to redo the design. He's stopping by tonight with the new plans and a revised budget." Anne thought for a moment and added, "And, I've canceled my trip to Italy."

"Italy?" CC asked.

"I was going there to pick out Carrara marble but I think I can settle for American granite instead."

"I'm glad you can make it work," CC said.

"We all have to make sacrifices," Anne said, not catching her friend's sarcasm. "Let's all go for a ride. We'll get breakfast."

"I just opened the store," CC said.

"Oh, yeah, that doesn't make sense. Someone should stay with the store. Ingrid and I will go." Before CC could argue, Anne was handing the keys to Ingrid and climbing into the passenger seat. Ingrid smiled and waved goodbye.

CC watched as the SUV that cost more than her first house turned the corner and disappeared into the mist.

Ingrid drove, adjusting the buttons on the stereo. "This is so sweet, Anne. Thank you for letting me drive."

"You're welcome. Thank you for keeping our secret," Anne said.

"Why are you being so secretive? CC would understand about the accident and that you needed a new car. Your car was trashed."

"I didn't want CC to know the circumstances leading up to the end of my Mercury Mystique. She would have lectured me about the brakes and vehicle upkeep. I didn't want to hear it."

"She does that because she cares about you. She does the same to me."

"I know that, and I love her, too. Part of the problem is I've been staying at her house for the past six months, and I have to tell you, she's not the easiest person to live with."

"That's funny. That's what CC said."

"Really? She did, did she? Hmmph." Anne paused. "Now that I've made my final decision about the house design, we can break ground. Hopefully I'll be moving out by the end of the year."

"I, for one, am sad to hear that. I've loved staying up late watching old movies with you on the couch, watching live auctions on the computer. You've taught me so much."

"Well, Ingrid, I wanted to surprise you. Originally I was going to build a small guesthouse in the back but even though I'm downsizing I'll still include a wonderful guest suite. You can stay anytime. Something overlooking the English garden."

Ingrid smiled. "That's so great, Anne. By the way, where are we going?"

Anne pressed a button on the large navigation screen. "It's already programmed in. Walker Brothers Pancake House in Arlington Heights."

When they arrived at the restaurant, Anne thought about the last time she'd seen the famous local logo, it had been at the original Walker's Brothers on Green Bay Road on Chicago's North Shore. That was the day she had traveled to Great-Aunt Sybil's house. She had the willpower that day not to stop but today was a celebration. A celebration of her newfound wealth, her new life and her new car. Her antique hunting skills had reaped a tremendous fortune.

After finding a parking spot in back, they waited in the line that stretched out the door. Anne tapped her foot, impatient as always. She could smell the hot maple syrup and she could almost taste the butter melting. At least that's what she thought. She knew the wait would be worth it. When they finally sat down at the booth, Anne squeezed in, the table pressing against her stomach. She glanced down. Had she really gained that much weight? She was only up maybe, one, well maybe two dress sizes. She was wearing her comfy jeans, the ones with the elastic around the waist and her silk tunic which didn't show much of her curves. Feeling the edge of the Formica rub against her belly button she realized she'd been dressing this way since her trip to Paris months ago. She had thrown caution and her diet to the wind. And she'd never gotten back on track. She let out a deep sigh.

"What's wrong?" Ingrid asked, perusing the menu.

"I don't know, Ingrid; I feel really fat." Anne was jealous, no envious, of the sweet girl sitting across from her with the body of a young Heidi Klum who could eat anything she wanted. At one time in her life Anne had been that girl but genes and time were unforgiving. Then she thought, *Jeans. I'm wearing elastic jeans. ohmigosh, this has to stop.*

"Don't be silly, Anne, in Germany or in fact anywhere in Europe, you know how many men would be pinching your behind?" Ingrid said. "My gosh, in Italy, you would be swarmed."

With that, Anne gave a bit of a smile. "I know it's not that bad. It's just." Out of the corner of her eyes, Anne saw a picture of Swedish pancakes smothered in lingonberries and whipped cream. Her other eye glanced at the table next to her that had just received their sausage and hash browns. She adjusted herself in the booth. "That's better." As the waitress came up to them, Anne pointed to the Swedish pancakes. "Oh, and hash browns, sausage patties, and a Denver omelet."

The waitress started walking away. "Wait, aren't you going to take her order?" Anne asked.

"Oh, I thought you ordered for the two of you," the waitress said.

"I'll have the Dutch baby pancake," Ingrid said.

The waitress started walking away again. "Oh, extra powdered sugar," Anne called after her. Anne put four spoonfuls of sugar into her coffee. Ingrid did the same. "I forgot to tell you last night because I was shaken up from the crash. It must have happened because I was distracted thinking about what Nigel told me at dinner," Anne said.

"What did he tell you?" Ingrid asked, clasping her coffee cup.

"Nigel received a call from the Glen Ellyn police about the woman who died at the store. Her name was Patricia Rounder."

Ingrid nodded her head, recognizing the name.

"It seems the car she was driving was stolen and she was wanted for murder in Ireland."

"Murder?" Ingrid's blue eyes grew wide.

"That's all the information Nigel had."

"What was she doing at the store? Why was she carrying that lantern?" Ingrid asked.

Anne perked up. "Lantern? That's right, the lantern. Where did I put it?" Anne thought for a moment. "It's in the trunk of my Mystique which is at the impound lot. I was going to take it to the police. I have to pay my tickets to get my car out of impound."

After they finished their breakfast, they headed back to Glen Ellyn. It was mid-afternoon, and the store was overflowing with customers. CC had a steady stream that she was ringing up at the counter. She glanced up as Anne and Ingrid came into the store. "It's about time you two got back. I've been swamped. I haven't had a break," CC scolded them. Ingrid took over the cash register. "There's someone here to see you," CC said to Anne, leading her to the back kitchenette.

"Anne, this is Catherine Henderson," CC introduced them. Anne stared at the old woman. She was dressed in jeans and a flannel jacket. Her gray hair was pulled back in a tight ponytail, her cheeks rosy, her eyes clear. "The police contacted Catherine about Patricia Rounder. They found her address in the GPS in the stolen car," CC explained.

"The police told me the whole story. You must have been traumatized." Catherine placed her hand on Anne's arm.

"Yes, it was horrible. I couldn't save her," Anne said.

"Did you know her?" CC asked Catherine, hovering over Anne's shoulder.

"No," Catherine said. "I never met her."

"Why do you think Patricia put your address in her GPS system?"

"I have no idea. I'd gone to town to pick up feed. When I got home, the police were waiting for me."

"Feed?" Anne asked.

"I have a farm up in Hampshire," Catherine said.

"Anne, the only two addresses the police found in the stolen car's GPS were Catherine's and our store," CC said.

"She came to see us. She must have been a fan. She was carrying a newspaper article about us and that old lantern," Anne said.

"Lantern?" Catherine asked.

"She was carrying an old kerosene lantern. She handed it to me right before . . ." Anne stopped, trying to be delicate. " . . . she passed."

"I'd like to understand why she had my address. What about this lantern? Why was it so important? Can I see it?" Catherine asked.

"That might be a problem." Anne glanced at CC, not quite ready to tell her about her accident. "I don't have it."

"What do you mean you don't have it?" CC asked.

"It's in my car," Anne replied.

"You car's out front," CC said.

"It's in my old car."

"Where's your old car?"

"CC, can we talk about this later?" Anne said. "Miss Henderson."

"It's Mrs. Henderson, dear, but call me Catherine, please."

"When I retrieve the lantern, I'd be glad to show it to you."

"That would be wonderful, dear."

"You know, Anne, Catherine's farm in Hampshire is called the Bee's Knees," CC said.

Catherine explained, "It's my organic bee farm. We raise free-range chickens, hormone-free cows and pigs. And, of course, we keep bees for organic honey. We also have a small café, real farm to farm table. I'd love to have both of you come out as my guests."

"That sounds delightful," Anne said, thinking about a cup of tea dripping with sweet honey. Maybe more honey than tea.

Catherine stood up. "By the way, I love your store. So many wonderful antiques. I have quite a collection myself, family heirlooms."

"Feel free to walk around," CC said. "Let me know if I can help you with anything."

"I will, dear, you've both been very sweet." Catherine grabbed CC's arm and kissed her on the cheek. Anne stood up and gave her a hug. Catherine gave them both a big smile and went back into the storefront.

"What a sweet lady," Anne said. "I have to get the lantern for her."

"What's stopping you, Anne?"

"There was a bit of a mishap last night."

"Let's make some tea and talk about it." CC put the teakettle on the small two-burner stove. After Anne told her the story about her car, CC sat for a few minutes while Anne went out to the front of the store to help Ingrid.

She pulled out her laptop and opened her blog. "Dear Friends," she typed. "Anne has bought a new car, SUV actually, and she has been actively, very actively, searching for items for our upcoming yard art sale. Here are some of the pieces she has found. I am particularly attached to this gate from an old church cemetery." CC posted a picture of the ornate wrought iron gate. "She has also found an amazing collection of garden pots, including this converted copper washtub." CC posted another photo.

"The linen sale was very successful. Thank you to everyone who stopped by. Also some very exciting news. DuPage County and the Glen Ellyn fire department in conjunction with my friend, Nick . . ." She stopped typing for a minute and then started again, "You've all seen photos of Nick and me out and about. We will be helping to start the Glen Ellyn Community Garden. The city has graciously donated four acres. I will be holding class Saturday morning for children, teaching basic planting skills and crop care. Each child will have their own sectioned area. Two of the acres will be reserved for the food pantry. We've also dedicated another acre to provide farm-to-table produce to area restaurants, all proceeds will help fund the community garden. Residents interested in having a section will pay a small fee. I think it's quite exciting.

"And on a special note, I've added pictures of some of the requested antiques we've found and shipped out to you, our friends. Maybe it will spark ideas for others who have not made requests yet.

"As I've promised, I've included one of my recipes. I'm working on my cookbook, hoping it will be available by Christmas. It will include holiday desserts and cookies and festive meals. Also, Anne will include some low-carb recipes. Here's one of them: Inside-out Chicken Parmesan

Ingredients

1-lb. skinless chicken breasts

2 cloves garlic

½ cup ricotta

1 cup mozzarella, shredded

1 cup parmesan, shredded

salt

pepper

Low-carb pasta sauce (Anne prefers four cheese)

Heat oven to 350. Cut a small pocket in chicken breast. Combine ½ mozzarella, ½ parmesan, ricotta. Heat 2 tablespoons of olive oil in cast iron skillet. Stuff chicken breast with ricotta mixture. Sear for 10 minutes on one side. Flip over. Pour pasta sauce on top of chicken, place remaining mozzarella and parmesan on top. Put in oven for another 10-15 minutes until chicken is done."

CC uploaded a photo of the completed recipe to accompany the blog. Then she closed her laptop.

Chapter Eight

"I need to pick up my car," Anne told the disinterested woman behind the sliding glass window. The large room outside the impound lot was grimy, Anne felt dirty just stepping inside.

"Driver's license, registration and insurance card," the woman behind the counter replied in a sing-song voice.

Anne rifled through her purse and dug out the required documentation. She slid them onto the stainless steel tray underneath the glass window. The woman picked them up and punched some keys on her computer with her long, exaggerated fingernails. Anne wondered how she was able to type. The woman frowned and then punched some additional keys with the knuckle of her index finger.

"What's going on? What's taking so long?" Anne asked. The line behind Anne was growing long and their patience growing short as they shuffled from foot to foot waiting for Anne and the sing-songy woman to finish.

The woman called over another woman who stared at the screen. The second woman turned to Anne and said, "You can't have your car."

"What do you mean?" Anne asked, her face turning red. Her breathing became rapid as she took shallow breaths.

"I mean what I said, we can't release your car to you until you go see the judge. You have outstanding tickets. When is your court date?"

"Next week but I need my car now," Anne said.

"You'll have to make other arrangements."

"I need to get a few things from the car. Can I at least do that?"

"I can't let you back in the yard, not until after your court date."

"You have to be kidding me," Anne said. "I can pay my tickets right now." She whipped her credit card out of her purse.

"It's too late to pay them here. You have to go in front of the judge."

"What do you mean?" Anne became more agitated. She counted to ten in her head but it wasn't working. It didn't slow her rapid breathing.

"Ma'am, you have to leave now." The uniformed officer waiting in the corner came over and told her.

"I just need a few things from my car," Anne repeated.

"You have to leave." The officer escorted her outside. He went back inside, leaving her stranded on the curb. Staring through the chain link fence, she could make out the bright green of her Mystique. She walked over, put her fingers through the holes of the links and looked up, as though she was thinking of climbing over the six-foot-high fence. And then she thought better when she saw the officer staring at her from inside the building. She turned on her heels and went to her Mercedes SUV.

Driving back to CC's, Anne tried to recall when she had received the tickets and how much she owed. This might mean the difference between her marble-topped vanity or laminate. She could see the dollar signs for her home flying out the window but she didn't see the flashing lights behind her. When she finally did, she pulled over to the shoulder. The officer came up to her window. "Officer, I wasn't speeding," she said, handing him her license and registration.

He came back a few minutes later. "It says here your license has been suspended due to your unpaid outstanding tickets. Also there is a warrant for damage of public property. I could take you in now but I'll let you off as long as you promise to appear at your court date, but you can't drive home. Is there someone you can call?"

"Officer, I'm okay. I'm just heading home. It's not very far. I promise I'll go straight home. Well, one stop at Saver's, there's a fountain I was looking at for our store. I decided to buy it. Oh, and then just a quick stop to Whole Foods for cookies. And then straight home, I promise," Anne said, smiling her brightest smile.

The office shook his head. "Ma'am, I've already called a tow truck. I can't let you drive."

Anne's day had gone from worse to worser. She picked up her phone and called CC.

A short while later, CC pulled up in the VW bus as the tow truck was leaving with Anne's new Mercedes SUV. "What happened, Anne? What's going on?" CC asked as Anne got into her car.

"They said my license is suspended. I don't understand it. I thought I paid all those tickets." Anne shoved the new tickets the officer had given her into her bag.

"Tickets?"

"I've gotten a few parking tickets in the city and other areas when I've been rushed doing my errands. I thought I paid them all but I must have forgotten a few. The officer said my license was suspended. He wouldn't even let me drive home."

"Oh, Anne," CC said. "Did you at least get the lantern?"

"No, they wouldn't let me take anything from the Mystique. I have to go to court next week." Anne glanced at her phone. There was a text from Terrence. "Can you drive me to my home site? There's some problem with the ground breaking."

"What's wrong?"

"Terrence didn't say. They were supposed to begin breaking the old foundation today. We have all the permits and utility lines marked. I don't know what the problem could be."

As they pulled up in front of Anne's former bungalow, they could see the slight figure of 75-year-old Grandma Jan, Anne's next door neighbor, known as the neighborhood watch—the woman who got things done on the block. She was wearing a hardhat and a reflective vest. She waved Anne over. Meandering around her feet was her kitten, Snowball, one of Sassy's litter. Grandma Jan picked up Snowball, rubbing her soft white fur. "Bad girl, Snowball. She's as bad as her mother. I can't keep her in the house, Anne. With all the construction, it's not safe for her out here. Let me put her back in the house and then I can bring you up to speed."

Anne glanced around at the construction site. The remains of her early 20th century Chicago red brick bungalow had been cleared away. Chunks of the old foundation were torn up and lay to one side. Workers sat leaning up against a bulldozer, smoking and drinking coffee. "Why is no one working?" CC asked.

"I don't know. We have to find Terrence," Anne said.

Grandma Jan came back and handed Anne a stone. CC studied it over Anne's shoulder. "That's an arrowhead, Anne."

"I know," Anne said. "But why are you giving it to me?"

"That's what they found when they dug out the old foundation," Grandma Jan said.

"I'm sure there's plenty of arrowheads around," Anne said.

"This one is rather special," CC said. "It's Winnebago. The Winnebago were part of the Sioux nation. They lived along the Atlantic coast. For many years they were pushed west until they reached the Wisconsin River," she added, always eager to share her wealth of knowledge.

"I don't need a history lesson, CC," Anne interrupted.

"Anne, this is what makes it such an important find. The Winnebago claimed this area for their hunting ground and their burial ground."

Anne immediately thought of the movie *Poltergeist*.

"It wasn't until 1833 when the first white settler, Hezekiah Dunklee came to Addison Township," CC continued, ignoring Anne's comment. "After traveling to Fort Dearborn for supplies, he followed the path made by General Winfield Scott's army on its way west during the Blackhawk wars. That trail is now Grand Avenue and extends throughout the county."

"So, what does that have to do with me?"

"Hezekiah had a son, Ebenezer. He was a Whig and the first abolitionist in the township. He also was friends with Abraham Lincoln and some say inspired Lincoln to abolish slavery."

"What does this have to do with the arrowhead and with me?" Anne asked again, barely hiding her impatience.

"DuPage County was promised to the Winnebago by Ebenezer Dunklee to remain with their people as a hunting ground and burial ground in exchange for helping the settlers hunt and track game. If your lot is on a burial mound, you're going to have a tough time getting permission to build."

"I don't understand?" Anne asked.

"The Illinois Human Skeletal Protection Act requires that all unregistered graves and mounds be preserved," CC said.

Grandma Jan grabbed Anne's wrist and led her down into the excavation hole. "Anne, meet our neighbor." From under the rubble and dirt, a human skull smiled up at Anne. She did not return the smile.

Chapter Nine

CC drove following Ingrid's directions as she checked her Google maps on her phone. Anne sat quietly staring out the window of the VW bus, native drums pounding in her head. In the past, those drums signaled the arrival of her on-again/off-again fling, Chief John Blackbear, the man who had rescued her and CC in the Smoky Mountains. Now those drums signaled the halt of her dream house. "CC, what's that building?" Ingrid asked, pointing out the window.

"That's Dank Haus. It's the German-American cultural center. You know, Ingrid, this area of Chicago, Lincoln Square, is very steeped in German culture. At one time, Germans represented the largest population in Chicago. Lincoln Square is still traditionally German. That park over there." CC pointed across the street. "That's called Kempf Plaza. That's where the old-fashioned Lombard lamp is. It was presented to Chicago in 1979 by its sister city of Hamburg."

"I've seen those lamps in Hamburg before, by the bridge," Ingrid said.

"Over there is the Brauhaus. They have great bratwurst and schnitzel and homemade soups." CC pointed out sights as she drove down the avenue. "That's the Lincoln Square mural. It covers 3,000 square feet and was designed and drawn by a Chicago portrait studio and painted by area high school students," CC said.

Ingrid stared at the German castle and the Cologne cathedral all depicted in the mural. "I'm starting to feel a bit homesick."

In the back, Anne said, "Can we stop at the Brauhaus for lunch? I could use a bratwurst." She imagined it drizzling with sautéed onions, sauerkraut and spicy brown mustard with maybe a side of potato pancakes smeared with sour cream or applesauce or, even better, both.

"After we meet with Kimberly," CC said.

"Kimberly's aunt's house is a block east of Western, off of Lincoln. If you turn here, we should be almost there," Ingrid said.

They stopped in front of the old gray stone two-flat. There was a dumpster in the driveway. The narrow street was lined with parked cars on both sides. CC maneuvered around, searching for an open space. Kimberly, the young woman Ingrid had met at the store, was waiting out front. She waved them over. "Ingrid, hi," Kimberly said. "You must be Anne and CC. I'm so happy to meet you two. I'm such a big fan. I missed you at the store. It was so crowded. I didn't want to bother you. You think I could get a selfie with the three of you before we go in?"

Anne perked up. She pulled her long blonde hair off her shoulder. She was glad she was wearing her new teal blue Vince lambskin leather jacket. It had been a deal she couldn't walk away from at the Sak's outlet though still slightly above her budget. "Wait," she said, running over to the side view mirror. She pulled out her lipstick from her large orange Prada bag. Ingrid ran up behind her, pulling her lipstick out of her small orange Prada bag. Anne adjusted her look. She patted underneath her chin—chins, ohmigosh. "Is that really me?" she asked out loud. She had gone back to wearing her normal jeans, no elastic. They were a bit snug but she was determined she would fit comfortably into them again. For a 43-year old woman, she still didn't look older than 30. *It was her Swedish blood, her Viking heritage, sturdy Midwest woman,* she thought. And then she saw Ingrid's reflection in the mirror. Somewhere between a runway model and an angel. She let out a low sigh. "CC, let's skip lunch," Anne said.

They gathered around and moved in close for the selfie. After they had taken the picture, Kimberly talked to them in hushed tones, "I have to warn you. My cousin Gertrude is inside. We've cleared out a lot of the junk and managed to box up the valuables. I told her you were coming and that you might want to run the estate sale for us. She wasn't pleased with the idea."

"Why not?" CC asked.

"I think once you meet Gertrude, you'll understand. She's a bit of a control freak."

They followed Kimberly into the house. It was cluttered with moving boxes stacked to the ceiling. They recognized Gertrude immediately. Her name fit her. She was a large 50-something woman with a commanding presence wearing a housedress, her hair tied up in two tight buns, her rosy cheeks and jowls jiggled as she spoke. "Is this them?" She stared at the Spoon Sisters up and down with a patronizing air.

"Gertrude, this is Anne, Ingrid and CC—the Spoon Sisters," Kimberly introduced them.

"Ja, Ja, I know you told me. Antique hunters, the Spoon Sisters blog," she spoke to Kimberly in German.

Ingrid interrupted, answering in German, "We don't mean to interfere. We're here to help."

Gertrude appeared surprised. "Sie Sprecht Deutsche?"

Both CC and Ingrid nodded.

"Well, then, unlike my cousin here, I don't believe we need outside help," Gertrude said, returning to English.

"We have an extensive fan base, many of whom live in the Chicago area," CC said. "I'm sure they would be interested in your aunt's collections."

"We will see." Gertrude went back into the kitchen and continued emptying cabinets.

Kimberly turned to the Spoon Sisters. "I apologize for my cousin. She is not what you would call a people person. Let's go to the apartment upstairs. My aunt rented out this floor. Most of her stuff is upstairs."

The second-floor apartment was completely stuffed with sixty years of memories. Anne was drawn to the drum table with its beautiful walnut finish and leather top. She thought about how it would fit perfectly into her new English craftsman house, the one that would be built above the haunted Indian burial ground. She shook her head to remove the image of the Winnebago on the warpath.

Ingrid sifted through boxes and opened drawers of a beautiful matching walnut armoire. Then she saw it—it being a black forest cuckoo clock. "CC," she called out.

CC didn't answer, she nodded her head. They both walked over to the tiny card table that held a collection of clocks, including wall clocks, mantle and an early 1970s cassette bedside clock and the cuckoo clock. "You can see we started organizing things by type. These are the smaller clocks," Kimberly said.

"This clock is beautiful," Ingrid said, turning the black forest carving over to see the deep wood grain. "This is a pre-World War II clock, isn't it?"

Kimberly nodded. "She brought that with her, along with the Hummels."

"Oh, the Hummels." Ingrid clasped her hands together in enthusiasm.

"I have those in the back bedroom here."

They all followed Kimberly, weaving through the boxes, floor lamps, box fans, pots and pans until they made it to the back bedroom. "This is the Hummel room," Kimberly said. The small 10 x 10 foot room contained a collection of more than 500 Hummels standing at attention. Some in original boxes, others carefully displayed on card table tops. Anne felt very large in this very small room. She moved carefully, not wanting to topple a figurine. Ingrid and CC walked directly to what appeared to be the older Hummels.

"Kimberly, are you familiar with the Hummel figurines?" CC asked, picking up and examining the marks on the bottoms.

"Not especially. I played with some of these when I was a little girl."

Anne's heart sunk thinking of a little girl playing dolls with these thousands of dollars worth of Hummels.

"The Hummel figurines are based on the drawings of a nun called Berta Hummel," CC said. "They were first produced by W. Goebel Porzellanfabrik of Oeslau, Germany, in 1935. The crown mark was used from 1935 until 1949. The company added the *B* marks in 1950. The full *B* with variations was used from 1950 to 1959." CC held up various statues looking for the different marks. "It makes it very easy to date Hummels according to their marking. Porcelain figures inspired by Berta's drawings were reintroduced in 1997. These are marked *BH* followed by a number. They were made in the Far East, not in Germany." CC picked up several of the Hummels and showed Kimberly the *BH* markings on the bottom. "Where are the Hummels your aunt brought from Germany? They should have the crown mark," CC said.

Ingrid and Anne joined in, lifting up Hummels and checking the markings. All of them were stamped with the *BH.* "I don't understand. This is her whole collection or at least everything we found," Kimberly said.

"You couldn't have played with these when you were little, they weren't produced yet. These are all from the late 1990s," CC said.

From downstairs, they heard a crash. They rushed down to find Gertrude picking up shards of a hand-painted Bavarian rose plate, and swearing in German. "Kimberly, are you done? There's real work you can help me with."

"I personally would be interested in the drum table and cuckoo clock," Anne told Gertrude.

CC sshed her. "We'd be glad to run an estate sale for you. It's not something we normally do but, because Kimberly is such a fan, we'd love to help out. We can categorize and price everything," CC said.

"Price everything?" Gertrude asked.

"Certainly. We're antique hunters. We know the value of every single piece in this house," Anne said, staring a hole into Gertrude.

Gertrude shifted her feet. "I don't think that's necessary," she tripped over her words.

"Why not? We'll make more money if we know the value of what we're selling," Kimberly said.

"As executor, that decision is up to me," Gertrude said.

"Perhaps we can see the rest of the Hummel collection and give you a fair value," CC said.

"What do you mean the rest of the collection?" Gertrude placed her hands on her hips.

Kimberly turned to her cousin. "What is she saying, Gertrude?"

"The collection of Hummels upstairs are not the ones your aunt brought from Germany," CC repeated what she had said upstairs.

"Is that true, Gertrude?"

Gertrude shifted her feet again. "Well," she stammered. "I put some away for safekeeping and some I'm sure she would have wanted me to have as the oldest niece."

"The trust states that all the proceeds should be evenly distributed over the seven nieces," Kimberly said.

"Yes, but I'm doing all the work," Gertrude said.

Kimberly grabbed Gertrude by the hand and pulled her into the dining room. She spoke softly. When they returned moments later, Gertrude said, "Yes, we would like your help with the estate sale and pricing all the Hummels." She walked out the back door onto the porch.

"What did you say to her?" Anne asked.

"I told her that I would call the rest of our cousins and they're all bigger and meaner than her," Kimberly said.

Chapter Ten

Anne prepared the sales table, setting the cash box in front of her while CC and Ingrid moved from room to room inspecting all the displays, making sure everything was priced and that the tags were visible. It was the second day of the estate sale in little Germantown. Gertrude had kept a close eye on Anne and CC during the previous day's sale, which had been quite successful.

A dealer had come in the first day and snapped up all the early Hummels. The only ones left were the 1990s non-German made statues. Gertrude did not put up a struggle parting with them. Three of the other cousins made sure of that. Other items had quickly been sold from the house, items that Anne hadn't seen the first time she'd been here. She'd been too busy to inspect any new finds herself and had to rely on Ingrid's eye. The Spoon Sisters had set aside a silver candelabra, picture frames and a stained glass fireplace screen depicting a peacock. Anne thought if they didn't sell in Great-Aunt Sybil's Attic, they would all fit nicely in her soon-to-built maybe home. Her plans for an English craftsman had been delayed again while she waited for an update on her petition to the city. "Hey, Ingrid, come here a second." Anne waved to Ingrid. "There's a German bakery right off of Western, not more than a block from here. Could you run over and get a box of strudel or cookies, that we could put out?" Anne handed Ingrid a wad of cash.

"Sure, Anne, but first if you have a minute, a couple of the fans wanted to get a picture with you," Ingrid said. "They have questions about authenticating a toy top."

Anne's eyes lit up. She had been collecting children's tops since she was a child going with her dad to estate sales. She had amassed quite a personal collection. "Where are they?"

"Over there." Ingrid pointed to the line quickly growing outside the door. Anne stepped out onto the porch. "This is her. This is Cindy, Anne."

A very petite and very pregnant dark-haired woman ran up to Anne and threw her arms around her. Anne beamed. "Ohmigoodness, Anne Hillstrom, I have read every single one of your blogs from day one. I was at the opening of Great-Aunt Sybil's. I didn't get to meet you because you were so busy. Is CC here, too? Do you think we could get a picture?"

"CC's off somewhere in the house. I'm sure we can find her," Anne said.

"I'm a little embarrassed to say I've started a Spoon Sisters fan club."

Anne pictured a lunchbox with the Spoon Sisters' likeness. Perhaps airbrushed slightly to hide her double chin. "Don't be embarrassed. That's wonderful," Anne said.

"It's kind of like a book club. We meet once a month, rotating houses and read the blogs while we drink tea."

"What a marvelous idea," Anne said.

"Everyone must bring a baked good."

"I'm liking this more and more," Anne said, picturing fresh baked shortbread or maybe even pecan tarts, warm and gooey from the oven. "Ingrid, bakery," Anne mouthed over Cindy's shoulder. Ingrid nodded and then ran off down the street.

"We also test CC's recipes. We particularly loved her shrimp scampi."

"Good news. We're working on a Spoon Sisters cookbook."

"That would be marvelous. Have you ever thought about opening a restaurant adjacent to the store?"

"The thought's crossed my mind," Anne said. She saw a cozy little shop with fresh pastries and hot tea.

"We're planning a neighborhood-wide garage sale. I'd love it if you could make a special guest appearance. The whole fan club would come. At our meetings, we discuss antiques, bringing in any finds or family heirlooms. I can't tell you how useful your tips on authenticating items have been. It's saved me making some bad buying decisions."

"Wow, this is so nice to hear. I can't tell you the weight that's on my shoulders. The responsibility involved with being an antique hunter," Anne said. "I'd be glad to come to your garage sale. I'm sure CC would, too."

"Thank you." Cindy pulled a children's top out of her coat pocket and handed it to Anne.

Anne studied it. It was a mahogany dancing top shaped like a turn-of-the-century woman with two spindles for arms. She spun it on one of the little wooden tables on the porch. "This is really cute. I'd say it's early 1900s. The one arm appears to have been repaired." She searched it for any markings or stamps. "I have one similar to this in my collection. I would put a value on it of $80. If it hadn't been repaired, it would probably bring another $40. Can you tell me the history behind it?"

"It was actually my great-grandmother's. It was one of the toys she played with when she was a little girl. I have a couple of her dolls and a whole trunk full of tops. Over the years, she collected some of the tops she had lost as a child," Cindy said.

"Did she grow up around Baltimore?" Anne asked.

"Well, yes, how did you know?"

"I'm not familiar with this particular top but its shape is reminiscent of a turnstile dress which was popular on the East Coast, especially in Baltimore, in 1903 and 1904. It was called a *turnstile* because of the way the bottom hem would float around when you spun in a circle."

"That's really interesting. I didn't know anything about the top other than it was my great-grandmother's."

"Did your great-grandmother live near the ocean?"

"Her father was a crab fisherman."

"I thought so. If you notice, there's a little symbol. It's faded but it was originally painted on the top." Anne took her flashlight out of her large orange Prada bag. "It's a picture of St. Peter. Fishermen carried the medallion as a talisman for good luck in their catch and for safety, especially at the turn of the century. It would make sense that a father would want to give his daughter a toy with St. Peter's blessing on it."

Cindy sat down on one of the folding chairs on the porch. She clutched her protruding stomach.

"Are you okay?" Anne asked.

"I'm getting very, very close."

"Can I get you some water?"

"I've been on my feet too long."

"Let me get you some water." Anne rushed into the house and came flying back out carrying a glass of water, spilling half of it on her way. She handed it to Cindy, who took a sip.

"See, Anne, this is why I started the fan club."

"Come by the store. Bring all your toys, and I will appraise them. We can put them on consignment if you want to sell them."

"What I'd really like is to trade them all for a Steiff bear like the one you found for Ida."

"Yeah, we could do that."

"I'm having a little girl. I thought that would be a neat tradition to start her down the trail of antique hunting."

"Yes, that's how I started." Anne's musings were interrupted by CC, who came out of the house.

"Anne, we were supposed to open already. And, where's Ingrid?"

"I sent Ingrid for treats for the guests. Oh, CC, meet Cindy, she's the president of our fan club."

"We have a fan club?" CC asked.

Cindy slowly lifted off the chair, hanging onto the porch railing. Anne held her arm to steady her. "Both Spoon Sisters, we have to get a picture." Anne looked around and saw Gertrude peeking out the porch window. She walked back into the house pulling Gertrude behind her. "Gertrude, please take a picture for us."

"Thank you; how soon until the sale starts?" Cindy asked.

"It's starting now. You're the first in line," Anne said, opening the front door after the picture had been taken. "Gertrude, I want you to walk around with Cindy and help her out. Make sure she has somewhere to sit and don't let her carry anything."

Gertrude turned red. She nodded and walked in behind Cindy.

"Anne, you're so bad," CC said.

"Oh, Gertrude deserves it," Anne said.

Cindy screamed as she entered the small house, a puddle appeared at her feet. "The baby!" she yelled.

CC rushed over while Anne dialed 9-1-1. "Come inside, sit down." She led Cindy to the old orange flowered camelback couch.

"Oh, it hurts so much," Cindy moaned, clutching her stomach,

"The ambulance is on its way," CC said, holding her hand.

"The baby's coming," Cindy said.

"Oh, no, you're just starting contractions there's plenty of time."

"No, I can feel it. I have to push." Cindy scrunched her face and pushed, crushing CC's hand.

CC glanced over her shoulder at Anne, who was flying through the front door. "They're on the way. I called," Anne said.

A short while later, Ingrid arrived with several boxes of pastries. Anne flung open a box and grabbed a cookie. "What's going on?" Ingrid asked.

"The baby's coming," Anne mumbled with a mouthful of cookie.

Cindy yelled again and squeezed CC's hand harder. "Where's the ambulance, Anne?" CC asked.

"Western Avenue is all backed up. There was an accident," Ingrid said.

Cindy screamed again. "It's coming. I know it's coming."

CC checked her watch, the contractions were a minute apart. The baby was coming. Like it or not, she rolled up her sleeves. She looked up at Ingrid and Anne.

"You're kidding? You're not serious?" Anne said.

"The baby's crowning," CC said. "Ingrid, get some towels."

As Cindy pushed, CC brought the baby into the world. She placed the baby girl on Cindy's chest and wrapped them both in a blanket as the paramedics burst through the door with a gurney. "We'll take it from here, ma'am."

CC backed away. Cindy smiled up at CC and grabbed her hand as she made the paramedics stop. "Wait, wait, thank you so much, CC. I want to name her after you. What does CC stand for?" Before she could answer, the paramedics wheeled her out.

After the paramedics left with Cindy, Anne and Ingrid tidied up the living room before reopening the sale. Items flew out of the house faster than Anne could ring them up. CC managed the sale in the garage, Ingrid took the top floor. By the end of the day, most everything was gone. CC wandered around, picking up stray items and boxing them either for their store or Goodwill. "Anne, I'm going to take one last walk around the garage before we lock up," CC said.

She went out into the detached garage in the alley behind the house. The floor was nearly empty except for a few stray oilcans, a bald tire and some old crown molding. CC examined the wood. It was original from when the house was built. Overhead in the rafters there were more pieces of the crown molding stacked. She admired the craftsmanship. She grabbed a milk crate from the corner and stood on it trying to reach the crown molding. She stood on her tiptoes. She pulled one piece, bringing the whole pile crashing down around her. She fell, landing on her back, covering her face. She hoped Anne hadn't heard the noise. She gathered up the wood and put it in a neat pile to use for her house. From underneath the pile, she made out a small leather case, no larger than a briefcase. She pulled it out. It was covered in cobwebs and dust. She examined the latches. They appeared to be gold plated and still in good working order. She pressed the buttons on the latches and opened up the case. Inside was a green velvet lining and lettering in gold reading,

"Marshall Field." Engraved on its lid was a depiction of the 1893 Colombian Exposition with the famous "Field" clock in the center. The base held two sets of playing cards and six rows of off-white poker chips and a flask. CC picked up one of the chips and rubbed it between her fingers. It was marked $100. "This looks like ivory," she murmured. She picked up one of the playing cards, checked its edges, it was gold leaf. She carefully closed the case and carried it into the house.

"What's that, CC?" Ingrid asked.

Anne glanced up, powdered sugar from the apple strudel covering her chin. She stared at the case that CC was carrying.

"I found this in the garage or, rather, it found me," CC said. She placed it on the card table, opened it up and turned it around so Ingrid and Anne could see its contents.

"These cards have gold leaf around the edges. I think the poker chips are ivory," CC said.

"Look at the initials on the flask. DJS." Anne said, holding the silver flask. "This is a very expensive poker kit. I wonder whose initials those are."

"I was wondering the same thing," CC said.

"It's definitely too expensive to be a souvenir from the exhibition," Anne said.

CC looked around. "Where's Kimberly?"

"She and Gertrude are locking up," Ingrid said. Gertrude entered the room, followed by Kimberly.

Kimberly sat at the card table and examined the card case. Gertrude stood in the corner with her arms folded, mumbling something in German. "Where'd you find this?"

"Out in the garage," CC said.

"It's the first I've seen of it. Our great-grandfather worked at Marshall Field. He was a custodian."

"Would he have worked there during the exposition?" CC asked.

"That sounds about right," Kimberly said.

"This does not look like something a custodian could afford. Even back at that time it had to cost hundreds of dollars," CC said.

Anne interrupted. "Do you know whose initials these are?"

"No, I have no idea." Kimberly shook her head.

"We're going to do some research. I think you'll get a good price for this. Speaking of which, you've done quite well the past few days."

"I really want to thank you for everything. All the cousins do." Kimberly stopped and looked over at Gertrude. "Almost all the cousins are very grateful."

Anne gave Kimberly a hug. "If it's okay with you, we'll take the case and we'll let you know what we find out."

Kimberly nodded.

Chapter Eleven

Small 1960s pillbox ranches turned into towering modern McMansions as the Spoon Sisters entered the affluent suburb of Hinsdale. The canopy of linden, ash and old-growth oaks ran the length of the main street. Anne and Ingrid had their noses pressed against the VW's windows admiring the magnificence of the limestone facades and beautifully manicured landscapes. "Our fan club must be well off," Anne said.

"Tell me more about this fan club. I feel a little uncomfortable having a fan club," CC said.

"CC, it's no different as having fans on our blog except we're meeting in person."

"No, I understand the concept, Anne, it's just the blog fans are fans of the Spoon Sisters and we're Anne and CC."

"I don't see the difference," Anne said.

"Anne, it's obvious. Our readers are fans of the Spoon Sisters, the fictional heroines of the blog, and we're real-life."

"Heroines?" Anne interrupted.

"No, by no means." CC shook her head. Anne wasn't getting her point.

"That's how I see you two," Ingrid said. "Even my friends back in Germany think you're special. You've become bigger than life."

Anne smiled. "See, CC, that's what I mean. We have a reputation to maintain."

"Okay, if you say so." CC stared straight ahead.

"Cindy's block is to the right after this next street. It's called Poplar," Anne said. "The church holds its rummage sale at the same time as the neighborhood holds its annual garage sale. All the funds go to the church."

"It's a good cause at least. I still feel a little uncomfortable," CC said.

"CC, it's gonna be a couple of fans who enjoy reading the blog and are antique enthusiasts. Not a big deal," Anne said.

CC turned the corner. All of a sudden, there were police barricades blocking off the street, which was filled with hundreds of people, snapping photos at the first sign of the VW bus. "Ohmigosh, Anne," CC said. Balloons decorated the lampposts. A big banner ran across the street. It read, "Welcome, Spoon Sisters."

Anne beamed. "This is great, CC." She stepped out of the VW, waving her arm in the air and holding up the large orange Prada bag. The crowd cheered. Many of them held up their own large orange Prada bags, most of them imitation. Anne's eyes welled at the sight. A fitting tribute to her beloved bag.

CC spotted flashes of pansy-festooned Capri pants. She rolled her eyes. She watched Anne weave her way through the crowd like the queen greeting her subjects. A little girl touched Anne's sleeve. Anne glanced down. "These are for you." The girl handed her a spring bouquet.

"Dakota," Anne said, recognizing the girl.

Dakota blushed. "You remember me?"

"Of course, I do. How is your doll?"

"Her name is Mabel, and she's my favorite."

Anne noticed her little orange Prada bag.

"It's not real, but do you like it?" Dakota whispered.

"I think it's fabulous." Anne bent down and posed for a picture with Dakota. She was reveling in the notoriety. When Cindy said their fan club was coming, she thought a few friendly housewives but never expected this type of crowd. Maybe all her sacrifices over the past few weeks—no make that months—were worth it. Parting with all her treasures and finding homes for them, each new fan she met told a tale of a find Anne had discovered and what it meant to them and their family. Anne was very proud of herself.

CC stood back before following Anne through the crowd. Fans stopped her, asking for her autograph. CC signed reluctantly at first but gradually got into the spirit and began bestowing advice. She was more than pleased to share her knowledge with their eager fans. Ingrid posed by the VW with some young girls her age. They exchanged antique hunting stories.

A small stage was set up halfway down the block with balloons. It was decorated with antique milk cans and pickle jars filled with wildflowers. Cindy parted through the crowd, coming up to Anne. She hugged Anne. "Cindy, how are you? How's the baby?"

"I feel great. My mom is watching her. I didn't want to bring her into this crowd."

"What is all this?"

"This is your fan club."

"The way you spoke, I thought maybe a couple friends dropped by for a glass of wine and to talk antiques. I didn't realize it was this big."

"I do a blog about your blog, I sent it to the rest of the fans on my fan site. I also told them we were having a garage sale and that you, Ingrid and CC, were coming. It snowballed from there. You think that you and CC could say a few words?" Cindy glanced over at the stage.

"Of course."

CC and Ingrid caught up to Anne. "CC, you remember Cindy? The president of our fan club? They want us to say a few words," Anne said.

"Of course, I remember Cindy," CC said.

"It's good to see you." Cindy hugged CC. "Baby Cecelia—Baby CC—and I have so much to thank you for."

CC thought to herself, *Should I tell her that's not what CC stands for?* Then she thought, *It's too late now. Why spoil it?*

"Can you say a few words?" Cindy asked again.

This was CC's moment. She could educate this entire crowd about antique history and the history of antiques. "Of course."

Cindy pushed Anne up onto the stage. Anne motioned for CC to join her. Cindy waved her hands to silence the crowd. "Thank you all for coming to the Poplar Avenue garage sale," Cindy said. "All proceeds benefit the Poplar Protestant Church. Of course, our special guests don't need any introductions. We're so happy to have them here on our little block to help us with our sale. Anne and CC—the Spoon Sisters."

The crowd cheered. CC pulled Ingrid up on stage. Anne tapped on the mic. "Is this working? Is this working?" It squealed. "Thank you for such a warm welcome. We're so happy to be here and to meet everyone. I recognize so many of you from your pictures on the blog and those of you who have come to the store. I want to let you know how much we care about you and your requests. More than I care about my own." Anne stopped for a moment and thought about her house currently on hold, her storage unit which held treasures yet to be discovered. "We share a love for lost treasures and the caretaking of history. Matching a loving family with an orphaned artifact is truly my passion and my life."

The audience applauded and rushed the stage as CC reached for the microphone. Anne and Ingrid left the stage with the crowd following them. CC stood awkwardly alone with only a little boy eating a snow cone. He looked up at CC and offered her a lick of his snow cone. She could see he felt sorry for her. She smiled and patted his head before following the crowd to where Anne and Ingrid were appraising items on a long folding table. Ingrid held up a porcelain figure of a woman wearing a yellow dress and hat. "This is a Dresden porcelain figurine made in Germany. There's a slight crack in the ruffle of the dress otherwise it is very lovely," Ingrid said.

The woman standing in front of Ingrid said, "Yes, that's 50 years old."

Ingrid noticed it priced at $40. "I really think it's worth twice that much, especially since it's for charity."

CC stood behind Anne and Ingrid, watching them. "Anne, what are you doing?" she asked as she saw Anne place several items including the Dresden figurine underneath the table.

"I'm taking these on consignment, CC. They're all nice antiques. I've worked it out. The consignee will get 60 percent and the store will get 40 percent." Anne held up an ornate orchid brooch. "I think this might be Lalique. I have to do some research." She placed it on her sweater, not able to resist it. "I might actually keep it myself."

"Anne, if that is Lalique it belongs in a museum," CC said. "And, between your house plans and the car, you don't have money. What about your house?"

Anne's face fell. Her dream house had become her albatross.

An older woman walked up and smiled at Anne. She handed her a curved, frilled painted bowl on a brass stand. Anne examined it carefully. "Can you tell me the story about this bride's bowl?" Anne asked.

The woman smiled. "It was a wedding gift to me and my husband."

"It's quite lovely. It's 19th century Victorian art glass. It's in very good condition," Anne said. She held it up for the crowd to see. "I believe the glass was made in Bohemia. Uranium was added to give it a luminescent quality. See how it glows even in the sunlight. The stand has angel's face and feet for legs."

Fans came one after another with their precious treasures. The pile under the table grew and grew. Ingrid broke off into her own little group and was lecturing on antique wooden jewelry boxes.

Cindy came up behind Anne and tapped her on the shoulder. "Anne, Pastor would like to meet you. He coordinated the garage sale with his annual rummage sale to draw a larger crowd."

CC took over at the appraisal table next to Ingrid. As Anne went down the sidewalk past the front lawns and driveways full of family castoffs, children's clothes, broken toys, she noticed Dakota following her. She stopped and turned around. "Dakota, do you need help with something?"

"Miss Hillstrom, I was wondering. I know that Ingrid is your apprentice and that she helps out at the store and everything. Miss Hillstrom, I was wondering if there'd be something around the store I could help with cleaning, polishing." The little girl asked hesitantly, holding her arms against herself.

Anne bent down eye to eye with Dakota. She felt her enthusiasm. "You do have the calling. The calling of orphaned artifacts?"

"Yes, Miss Hillstrom, I really do. I love discovering lost treasure and holding history in my hand." As she spoke, she opened her hand, which had been in a tight fist revealing an old silver dollar. She handed it to Anne.

Anne read out loud, "1893. Dakota, this is a Morgan silver dollar. Where'd you get this?"

"I found it."

Anne flipped it over. It was stamped "CC" for Carson City, Nevada. The last year that the Carson City mint issued coins. "Where'd you find this?"

"I found it in our basement when we were moving. I was helping my mom pack up."

"Oh?"

"My mom said the house was too expensive and we had to move."

"Where did you move to?"

"For a while, my mom and I stayed at a family place. Yeah, lots of families, when they're moving, they can stay for free."

"Like a shelter?" Anne asked. "Is your mom here?"

"Yes, I begged her to bring me. We took a bus from Chicago."

"Is that why you want to work at the shop? To make money?"

"I want to help. I want to learn, Miss Hillstrom."

"Call me Anne, please, call me Anne."

"When I came to your store, you know that $8 I saved, I saved it by working around the neighborhood helping rake lawns. I walked dogs. I tried to give it to my mom but she wouldn't take it. She wanted me to buy something at your store. She knew how excited I was to meet you."

Anne turned her head for a moment. She was overcome; she was holding back her tears. "Let's find your mother."

"She's sitting at the corner on the bench." Dakota pointed, waving to her mom.

Holding Dakota's hand, Anne walked over to a young woman in her late twenties with mousy brown hair wearing jeans and a t-shirt torn in a few spots. She had Dakota's look and smile. The same soft blue kind eyes as her little girl. Anne introduced herself and sat down next to her.

"Miss Hillstrom, has Dakota been bothering you?"

"No, of course not, she's a wonderful little girl."

"I'm Caroline," the woman said.

"Dakota told me that the two of you enjoy antique hunting."

Caroline smiled. "That's what Dakota calls it. It's really more rummaging."

"Antique hunting. Rummaging. It's all the same. It's finding use in things that don't seem useful. Value in things that seem to have none. Purpose in things that have lost their way."

Caroline smiled again. "I never quite thought about it that way, Miss Hillstrom."

"Call me, Anne."

"Dakota wanted to see you again but we need to get going."

Anne handed the Morgan dollar to Caroline. "Did you know about this?"

"I don't know what you're talking about." Caroline stared at the coin.

"Dakota says she found it."

Caroline looked over the coin. "It's obviously old. Is it worth anything?"

Anne looked it up on her iPhone. "It has value. Even a Morgan dollar in poor condition is worth at least $600."

"Really? I . . ."

"This coin is in very good shape, not near mint," Anne interrupted. "I would have it appraised. I think it's worth in the thousands."

Caroline sat back down on the bench and stared at the coin. "Dakota, where'd you find this?"

"Mommy, when I was going through the basement before we moved I was checking all the corners and the drawers in the furnace room like you asked. I found this coin in the back of one of the old wood drawers right next to the furnace where all those rusty tools were."

"How come you never showed it to me?"

"I wanted to ask Miss Hillstrom, I mean, Anne, what she thought it was worth. I wanted to surprise you. I thought maybe we could buy our house back and move back home."

Caroline pulled Dakota to her chest and hugged her. She looked up with tears in her eyes at Anne. "It's been a rough year," she whispered.

Anne sat back down next to the two of them. She put her arm around them. "Look, I have to talk to CC, but her ex-husband owns a lot of fixer-upper properties. He has an apartment building not too far from our store, one and two bedrooms, very nice. I think that maybe if you sell the coin, we could find a nice apartment for you."

Dakota smiled. "Do you think I could help out at your shop? Is it close to there? Can I walk?"

"Now, Dakota, don't impose on Miss Hillstrom."

"No, it's not imposing," Anne said. "Are you working?" she asked Caroline.

"I'm in between jobs right now. I've been looking but haven't found anything. I have no work experience and just my GED. I've only been able to find minimum wage jobs," Caroline said.

"Daddy left," Dakota said.

"That's settled. I'm making an executive decision. I think we have enough work for both of you at the store," Anne said. "Come see us on Monday, and we'll work out the details."

## Chapter Twelve

"Dear Friends," CC typed. "Anne and I had the pleasure of being invited to the Poplar Avenue garage sale in Hinsdale. It was nice to meet so many members of our fan club in person. Meeting you all makes what we do so rewarding. Hearing your stories, sharing information about history, talking history." CC paused, sipping her black coffee. "This brings me to our exciting news—Anne and I are branching out. We are helping a friend find antique linens for a wedding she is planning at the Sanfilippo estate in Barrington. If you know of any fine old linens, please let me know.

"Anne continues to work on plans for building her new house. She has had to scale back slightly due to unforeseen circumstances.

"We've had such a great response for our recipes. Anne and I are collaborating on a cookbook tentatively titled, *The Spoon Sisters Cozy Cookbook*.

"Your tips for the day: How to score at garage sales.

1. Start online the night before. Check out local listings and websites for that weekend's sales.

2. Map out your route to maximize your shopping. The more sales you can hit the better, so you can get a great deal.

3. Pick your area. If you're looking for antiques or furniture, you're better off searching in older neighborhoods.

4. Pack supplies including good magnifying glasses, a tape measure to measure the dimensions of larger items, shopping bags, newspapers to wrap fragile items,

cash—mostly $1 and $5 bills. The smaller increments give you more opportunity to bargain. Look for moving sales, and, as we have said in the past, your smartphone is your best friend. If you find an item you're not familiar with, click on eBay to get a general idea of what similar items are selling for. Oh, one last thing before I go, we hope to see you out at Great Aunt Sybil's Attic this weekend. We're having a fan appreciation day with treats and treasures. Hope to see you there." CC paused from typing, hoping she could persuade Anne to part with some of the treasures. "Until next time, dear friends."

Chapter Thirteen

Anne rushed into the courtroom. She had only meant to stop at the estate sale for a brief moment on her way but had been transfixed by a stunning silver tea service that would be perfect on the round drum table she'd bought from Kimberly's estate sale. With all the antique Hummels priced correctly, the sale had been a success, and her share of the proceeds was burning a hole in her pocket so she'd had to stop. Now onto the business at hand—paying her tickets, getting her Mercury Mystique out of impound, retrieving the lantern and—most importantly—getting her driving privileges restored. She already missed her Mercedes SUV that was parked in CC's garage. Uber drivers didn't appreciate having to share space with her finds.

The DuPage County courtroom was crowded. She sat on the hard wooden bench and tried to follow the activity at the front. Names were being called, people were standing in front and then they left. When it was her turn, she stood in front of the judge as the bailiff handed the judge her paperwork.

"Miss Hillstrom has eight outstanding parking tickets, two moving violations including one for obstructed vision and destruction of public property," the prosecutor said, checking his notes.

"I object," Anne said.

"Miss Hillstrom, you can't object," the judge said.

"Destruction of public property?" Anne asked.

"She destroyed a safety barrel on I-355," the prosecutor said.

"That was an accident. My brakes went out."

"That's here, too, driving an unsafe vehicle."

"How do you plead?" the judge asked.

"Not guilty, your honor."

"The judge gave her a questioning look. "How can you plead not guilty to all these violations? You're clearly responsible."

"There are mitigating circumstances."

"For instance?" the judge asked, tipping his glasses to the edge of his nose, looking at Anne as though he had already made up his mind.

"For instance, that ticket on the 19th was the day of the 40 percent off sale at Nordstrom Rack, which is usually 60 percent off already so I figured that it was 100 percent off. I ran in for one thing and left a note on my car. You can imagine how crowded the parking lot was on a Saturday and then *this* ticket." Anne grabbed it from the prosecutor's hand. "I remember this. It was in March. There was an estate sale on Clark in Chicago. Have you ever tried to find parking in Chicago on a busy street? As for the obstructed view, I could see just fine, and I was moving a sewing cabinet to my storage locker."

"You seem to be preoccupied with shopping," the judge said.

"That's my job. I'm an antique hunter. Not having my license keeps me from making a living which, I believe, is my constitutional right along with the pleasure I get from shopping for antiques—that's pursuit of happiness, isn't it? As far as liberty, you've taken away my freedom to go shopping." Anne didn't mention her ability to continue shopping on eBay and other online outlets.

The observers in the courtroom laughed, the judge banged his gavel and groaned. "Miss Hillstrom, that is a very colorful argument but I'm afraid none of it is relevant to your case. I think your behavior warrants more than a simple fine. You believe yourself above the law and I don't think paying a fine will teach you a lesson. I'm sentencing you to a hundred hours community service."

"What?" Anne's face grew pale. "But. . ."

The judge banged his gavel again. "See the clerk. Dismissed."

Anne stood still with her mouth open, staring around the courtroom for help. The bailiff walked over and escorted Anne to the clerk. "Miss Hillstrom, he'll help you pay the fines and set you up for community service."

Anne wrote a check for her fines and then studied the list of community service options that the clerk handed her. Picking up garbage on the roadside, cleaning out cages at the animal shelter, painting over graffiti, raking senior citizens' lawns. Anne plopped down on the hard wood bench. Her house was on hold and now her life was on hold. A hundred hours seemed like a lifetime. What about her real job? What about the orphaned artifacts found and yet to be found? Placing these homeless antiques with good homes—wasn't that community service? That's when she saw it— volunteering at the Treasure House. It was one of her favorite resale haunts. She had spent many hours there on the opposite side of the counter, looking for collectibles, household goods, books and baby shower presents. All the proceeds benefited the hospital and it might, over time, benefit Great-Aunt Sybil's Attic. It was perfect. She would be able to inspect items as they were brought into the store. Community service at its finest. She circled it and filled out the form to give back to the clerk. He handed her a timesheet, her driver's license and a receipt. "Bring this to the impound and you'll be able to retrieve your car."

Anne clicked her Uber icon on her phone. Even the thought of the Uber driver couldn't burst her new found joy. Things were coming together. While she waited on the bench in front of the courthouse, her phone rang. "Hi, Terrence," Anne said.

"Anne, a bit of some bad news from the archeologist. Your site and the skull that was found on it proves that your house was built on a Winnebago burial mound."

"How is that possible? The house was built in 1910. What about my neighbors' houses?"

"Your lot protrudes into the forest preserve and from the records that were available when your neighborhood was built, it appears your lot is the only one that was used by the Winnebagos."

"What do we do now?"

"We have a cease and desist order from the state while they send out a team of archeologists and officials to investigate it."

Anne's heart sank. "Where does that leave me?"

"And you'll have to pay for the excavation."

Anne stomped her foot. "That's not very fair."

"I'm sorry. We're way past fair," Terrence said.

"Where am I supposed to live? How long will this take?"

"At least six months to a year for just the excavation and then there will be the court hearing. Even if you are approved to build on the site, most of your budgeted building costs will be gone."

"Thank you, Terrence." She hung up. The Uber driver pulled up in his Ford Fiesta and honked loudly. The wind had been knocked out of Anne. Staying with CC another year. Anne shook her head and squeezed into the back seat. The driver played some horrible thumping techno music out of the little tin speakers. She started to open her mouth to complain but gave up.

They arrived at the impound lot. "Wait for me; I should only be a few minutes," Anne said, getting out of the car.

This time she showed the receipt showing that she had paid her fines and was able to retrieve her keys. She arranged to have a tow truck pick up the car to donate to cars for kids. The rest of the car's contents, a 13-pack of paper towels, two 40-pound bags of kitty litter, a copper birdbath, a box of mason jars and the lantern all stuffed into the Fiesta trunk and backseat. The Uber driver tried to complain but Anne was in no mood for his nonsense. They reached CC's Glen Ellyn split-level as the sun was setting. The Uber driver helped Anne unload. Well, not really help—he actually threw most of Anne's things onto the lawn and then took off in a huff. Anne glanced up at the split level as the sun set. Another year.

Chapter Fourteen

Anne stared into the bay window of the store. She had spent the morning arranging the collection of Hummels that hadn't been sold at Kimberly's aunt's estate sale. Sassy sat on the edge of the window seat, waiting for the opportune moment to slalom through the figurines with her kitten, Sybil, close behind her. They continued their way through the Hummels until a little yellow finch flew onto the feeder on the front porch. Anne reached out to grab them both before they could knock over any of the figurines. The pieces weren't her favorites but she didn't want to have to pay to replace them. As she grabbed the Persians, she saw a red panel van pull in front of the former sweet shop next door.

That wasn't the alarming part. It was *who* stepped out of the truck. There he stood in the late spring early Saturday morning sunshine in all his glory. Dirty overalls, greasy hair or what was left of it, scratching his grizzly white beard. John James Reeney, the ex Mr. CC. *Ohmigosh,* Anne thought. What's he doing here? she asked Sassy.

Sassy's response was to leap out of her arms and slip out the front door with Sybil hot on her heels. She leapt onto the finch feeder like a trapeze artist. Sybil jumped after her, grasping onto Sassy's bottom paws, the two cats dangling in mid-air. Anne walked out onto the front porch just as a flatbed hauling lumber and boxes pulled up. John Reeney unlocked the door to the sweet shop and all Anne could hear was a swear word, something drop, another swear word and "I hear you."

Anne watched throughout the morning, hearing the occasional crash followed by cursing. CC and Ingrid pulled up a short while later, unable to park in front of the store which was now blocked by all the construction vehicles. When CC saw Blue Chip Construction on the panel van, she shook her head. Anne was waiting on the porch, rocking, and sipping tea. Sassy was licking her wounds. Sybil was begging for a cookie off the tray Anne had set for herself. "When did this all happen?" CC asked.

"They showed up early this morning. They've been working on the sweet shop for the last few hours," Anne said.

Ingrid flipped the open sign in the front window of the store. Customers filed past Anne, who clung to her rocking chair, exhausted from her recent ordeals but not too exhausted to give a hug or take a selfie even though her heart wasn't in it. When John James Reeney was involved in a project, trouble followed.

Crossing the side yard, CC stuck her head in the front door of the former sweet shop. The room was full of dust as electrical saws whined and hammers pounded. Through the chaos, she saw the back of a baseball cap, popping up and down from behind sheets of drywall. John James Reeney peeked over the top. He wore a dust mask with a hole cut through the center and a cigar sticking out. He saw CC and came over to her. "Yeah, how you doing there? Let's go out front. It's dusty in here."

They stepped onto the front porch. "John, what's going on here? Did you buy the building?" CC asked, staring at all the commotion going on around her. She thought she had finished with his fix-it-up projects when he moved out. Now she was surrounded again. She kicked at the nail gun sticking straight up on the wood porch.

"Nah, I'm fixing her up."

"For who?"

"For a real estate broker who's flipping it. He's got a buyer but they want it fixed up first."

"Oh," CC said.

"All hush hush." John laughed his piercing, headache inducing laugh. The laugh that had finally caused CC to let him and their marriage go about seven years ago. She had tried. Lord knows, she had tried for 15 years. She had gotten past the maxed-out credit cards, rotating jobs, muddy boots all over the carpet, the I'll-get-around-to-its, the constant mess, the thoughtless missed birthdays and anniversaries, the exploding water heaters— but that laugh was the final straw. Even now it gave her a migraine.

"I hope they open a nice store. It'll help us," CC said.

"How's that going? That little antique business? I was thinking you might want me to bring over some of my stuff and, like, you could sell it for me."

"Sure, John, be glad to do that."

"Your store looks good. It was a nice property. I hated to give it up. I was getting around to finishing it."

Like the other 20 projects that never got finished. She didn't have high hopes for the building next door, the one currently occupied by Great-Aunt Sybil's attic until she and Anne had taken it over. "John, we have a lot of customers. I have to get back to work," CC said.

"Yeah, I hear you." His laugh followed her as she headed back to Great-Aunt Sybil's Attic.

From her vantage point on the porch, Anne watched the whole exchange. CC had that look, the look that Anne hadn't seen in a long time. The John James Reeney look, a mixture of exhaustion, depression and hopelessness. "Hey, Anne, do you mind if we close early today? I need to get away," CC said.

"Whatever you need, CC."

After they locked up the shop, they drove out to Catherine Henderson's house. Anne held the lantern on her lap, protecting it as CC drove along the bumpy, rural road. They passed by farmettes, new cookie-cutter homes and then came to a split rail fence with a hanging sign reading Bee's Knees Organic Farm. They drove down the path and pulled up in front of the farm stand. Several cars were parked in front. People browsed through the bins of early-season vegetables and preserves. There were also infused olive oils and stacks and stacks of honey. Behind the outdoor counter stood Catherine Henderson. She was in her flannel shirt, rolled up sleeves, her floppy gardening sunhat. She painted the picture of a gentlewoman farmer. She smiled warmly at all the Chicagoans who had made the trek out for locally sourced organic fruits, vegetables and honey.

Catherine came out from behind the counter and hugged Anne, then Ingrid, then CC. "I'm so glad you came. Let me show you around." She motioned to one of her assistants to take over the cash register. They strolled down the aisles and the loaded bins. "I'm sorry but it's still too early for anything except early girl tomatoes and all our preserves. I do have some pork and steak that we had frozen."

"This is really nice. I never knew you were up here. I always try to use locally sourced and organic foods. I grow a lot in my own garden," CC said.

"Oh, you're a gardener. Let me show you our greenhouse." They crossed the compound to a large glass enclosed building. Inside was a collection of vegetables. "Everything in here—the asparagus, the cauliflower—is pesticide free." They reached the back of the building; there was a large fish pond. "We do organic hydro-farming. The fish poop in the water and then the water's filtered through the dirt and it fertilizes the plants."

"This is amazing. I've thought about doing more self-sustaining gardening." CC saw a red-haired man putting leftover table scraps into a compost bin. "Is that compost for the greenhouse?"

"No, he's feeding the earthworms. The earthworm trailings are excellent fertilizer, full of nitrates," Catherine said.

"Yes, earthworms are an excellent sign of a healthy garden," CC said.

"This is my nephew, Sean. He helps out on the farm." Catherine called, "Sean, come over. I want to introduce you."

He set down the pail and limped over.

"Your leg still bothering you?" Catherine asked.

"It feels better," Sean said.

"Sean does everything around the farm. He's been working on irrigation ditches for the crops. He's built a rainwater capture system, part of our self-sustaining farming."

"Nice to meet you, Sean," CC said.

Sean took his glove off and shook CC's hand.

Anne knelt down by the section of herbs and smelled the thyme, cilantro and fresh basil. They walked out the back, which opened to a large 40-acre field. "We have open grazing for the cows. We churn our own butter and make our own cream. The back ten will be late summer sweet corn," Catherine said. "We have kale over behind that field. In the far field we grow crops for the local food pantry."

"That's a wonderful idea. We're starting a community garden in Glen Ellyn," CC said.

"That's wonderful, dear. I have so much land left. I'd love to help out anyway we can."

"Maybe we can take a day trip out, especially with the kids, to show them a real working farm."

Catherine smiled. "Yes, let's make a day of it. I think it's a shame that they don't teach real-life skills in school anymore, whether it be farming or carpentry. Things I learned from my father growing up."

"I agree. There's nothing like feeling the accomplishment of building something with your own two hands," CC said. "Or feeling dirt between your fingers."

"That's settled then. We're going to do this, aren't we, CC?"

CC smiled. A chicken pecked at Anne's foot.

"That's Henrietta, don't mind her. All my chickens are free range. Where are my manners? You all must be hungry after your drive out here."

Anne hadn't mentioned it but she was famished.

"Let's go into the house. That's where the café is." The turn of the century white frame house looked like the house from *Field of Dreams* set against a beautiful open field of wildflowers and cornstalks. The front porch that wrapped around the house was decorated with cornstalk dolls and several rocking chairs of assorted sizes. At the corner of the porch was a hanging double swing. Anne and Ingrid ran over and sat on it, swinging and giggling. CC admired the craftsmanship of the house. Even though it was in need of repair the bones were solid.

"Please come in. I've made goat cheese-stuffed chicken breasts," Catherine said. They followed her into the kitchen. She served up four plates and sat at the long farm table with them. Windows faced the gardens.

CC bit into the savory chicken breast oozing with butter and lemon juice. The goat cheese melted onto her tongue. "Mmm. This is so good," she said. "I make a similar dish with mozzarella."

"Everything is from the farm. I make the goat cheese, the chickens are here and I grow the lemons in the hot house."

"Can I get the recipe?"

"Sure, I'll write it down for you. It's really easy."

Anne took a slice of the fresh baked still warm bread and slathered on butter and honey. She took a large bite. "Ohmigosh, this honey is too die for. It's so sweet and fresh."

Ingrid glanced up after finishing her second goat-cheese stuffed chicken breast. "How'd you come up with the name Bee's Knees?"

"My family had a dairy farm in Chicago back in the 1800s. They moved out here after the Chicago fire. My twice-removed grandmother started this farm. The family eventually raised pigs and grew vegetables in the 1920s. That's when they started growing corn."

CC smiled. "To make corn mash for whiskey?"

Catherine smiled. "Yes, I do have some black sheep in the family. During Prohibition, corn and bootleg whiskey was the main crop. They started keeping bees to sweeten the whiskey. They named the farm the Bee's Knees because it was a popular saying back then for the best of something."

"That's so cute," Anne said. Then she remembered the lantern. "I forgot." She jumped up from the table and ran out to the VW. She grabbed the lantern and then ran back into the farmhouse. "I brought this for you." She handed Catherine the lantern left by the late Mrs. Rounder.

"This is really wonderful," Catherine said.

For the first time, CC examined the lantern. "This is really interesting. It's an early hot blast tubular lantern by Dietz. They made the first ones around 1868. With hot blast lanterns, fresh air enters the base through the openings in the globe plate. The flame heats the fresh air and combines it with the compressed gas. This mixture passes into the canopy and through the side, supplying the flame."

Anne buttered up another slice of bread as CC continued, "Its design produces a steady yellow flame and the burning time is 10 percent greater than a cold blast lantern."

"CC, it's a neat old lantern. Simple enough," Anne said. "We don't need a history lesson."

CC gave her an irritated glance. "Maybe you don't want a history lesson but maybe Catherine wants to know where the lantern came from." She held up the lantern. "Here's the interesting part. The lantern is definitely from the mid-1800s but this elaborate scrollwork was not part of the original design. See these delicate lace etchings. It's like a sleeve placed over the bottom of the lantern. There's a keyhole in the sleeve, but the key seems to be missing. I don't understand why but this has definitely been modified. The original lantern was a very utilitarian design meant for the working man. The scrollwork was added later, maybe during the 1930s, from the look of the keyhole."

She tugged on the sleeve but it wouldn't budge. She handed it over to Catherine, who placed it on the table in front of her. "It's quite lovely. I'd love to have it for my front porch, but it was obviously so important to Patricia. "

Anne hesitated for a moment and then looked at the worry lines in Catherine's face. "You've been through a lot."

"We all have, dear."

"Yes, but I think the lantern would look marvelous on your porch."

"Anne, did poor Patricia say anything about the lantern? Anything at all? Or why she gave it to you?" Catherine asked.

Anne thought for a moment. So much had happened since poor Patricia. "No, I'm so sorry, Catherine. Have you heard anymore from the police?"

"Nothing after the funeral," Catherine said.

"You went to her funeral?" CC asked.

"I felt sorry for her, dying in a strange country with no family or friends."

"Even though she was a criminal?" Anne asked.

"Oh, dear, I'm sure she was desperate and in dire straits. I've been through hard times myself. I'm sure we all have. As you can imagine, there was no one else at the service."

"I understand that Patricia was visiting America," Anne said.

Catherine put her hand on top of Anne's. "Oh, sweetie, it's so nice of you to put it that way. Patricia was a fugitive. The police didn't say much about her circumstances but that she was wanted."

"Excuse me, can I use your washroom?" CC asked.

"Sure, dear, it's down the hall. First door on the right."

CC went down the narrow hallway that was lined with family photos. When she saw an old wooden frame containing a front page from the *Chicago Tribune,* she stopped to read the headline. The newspaper was dated 1997 and had a banner headline that read, "Chicago City Council Exonerates Catherine O'Leary."

She went back to the kitchen. "I see you're a history buff. That's an interesting story. I actually know the reporter."

"Which one is that?"

"The story about Mrs. O'Leary and the Chicago fire."

"That's a bit of my family history. All my Irish relatives are O'Learys."

"O'Leary?" CC asked.

"Yes, that O'Leary. That's my maiden name," Catherine said.

"I'm sorry. What are you two talking about?" Ingrid asked.

"According to legend, Mrs. O'Leary owned a dairy farm southwest of today's Loop area," CC said. "Her cow allegedly kicked over a lantern and started the Great Chicago fire on October 8, 1871."

They all stared at the lantern which was sitting in the middle of the table.

CC laughed. "It's an urban fairy tale. There was no lantern."

"Yes, a fairy tale, but nevertheless, my great-great grandmother was forced out of Chicago with death threats. She refused to return to Ireland with the rest of the family. Instead she came here to Hampshire."

Ingrid, CC and Anne became quiet and stared once again at the lantern.

Chapter Fifteen

Pushing Bandit back, CC opened the door to see a deliveryman, holding a clipboard. He thrust the clipboard at her. "I need a signature. We have a delivery for Anne Hillstrom."

"What?" CC stared at him. She walked toward the stairs and called up, "Anne."

Anne flew down the stairs. As CC followed Anne, she stubbed her toe on Anne's bookcase, which had landed in the middle of the living room. "It's here," Anne exclaimed. She signed the delivery receipt as two men carried in an oak mission-style brown leather couch. "I forgot I ordered this. It was so long ago." She directed the men to place it in the middle of the living room.

"Anne, what is this?" CC asked, staring in shock.

"I bought it for the man cave in the basement of the new house," Anne said, running her hand along the leather.

"Man cave? The house is only for you. Don't you need a man to have a man cave?" CC asked, putting her hands on her hips.

"I wanted to make the house comfortable for when I have guests. When Nigel comes over or when John Blackbear is in town," Anne said.

CC sighed, staring around the room, taking in the boxes, droppings and clutter. There were dirty clothes that had never made it downstairs to the laundry, piles of mail that hadn't been opened, empty glasses on her end tables and now this couch. "I can't take it anymore," she said.

"I never meant for it to wind up here," Anne said. "I ordered it months ago. Now with the delay of the house . . ."

"What do you mean, delay? It's never going to be built and you're never going to move out."

"I didn't know I was such a bother." Anne sank down onto the couch feeling the leather. "It's really soft."

"I don't care about the leather," CC exploded as Ingrid came down the stairs.

"What's going on?" she asked.

"I'll tell you what's going on. Your cousin and my best friend is kicking me out onto the street," Anne said, staring up at Ingrid, tears in her eyes.

"I never said that," CC said.

"You know, CC, you're not so easy to live with, either. Everything has to be in its place, everything has to be done on your schedule and if I get one more history lesson about the origins of carbon paper or why toothpicks are shaped like they are. Or . . ."

Ingrid stepped in front of Anne. "Stop. Both of you, stop. I can't believe such good friends can talk to each other like this." She paused a moment. "Grab your jackets. We're going for a ride."

CC and Anne obeyed Ingrid and followed her out to Anne's Mercedes. She drove the short distance to the store. "What are we doing here?" CC asked.

"Wait, you'll see." Ingrid opened the front door and led them up the staircase to the attic. She opened the door and turned on the lights. The area had been dusted out, cleaned, painted. The original hardwood floors had been refinished. The fireplace brick had been tuck-pointed. A stained glass peacock fire screen covered its front. Two red leather wingback chairs bordered the fireplace which had barrister book cases built in on either side. A 1920s swag alabaster floor lamp stood in the corner. A small kitchenette had been constructed in one corner with a granite countertop, an island and stainless steel appliances.

"What is all this?" CC asked.

Ingrid took them by the hand and led them into a small room behind the living room. It was a cozy bedroom with a four-poster Barrett bed and waterfall dresser. A bathroom was tucked in the corner and there was a small walk-in closet. "Who did this?"

"It was to be a surprise. Adam and I and some of his friends have been working on this for months."

"When? How come you never told us?"

"We came over at night after the store closed," Ingrid said.

"It's absolutely adorable," Anne said. She lay down on the bed and glanced into the open door. "Is that a bear claw tub?" She went into the bathroom. Anne sat down in the large porcelain tub. Above it, a skylight let in the aqua blue sky.

"Anne, this is all for you," Ingrid said. "Or at least until your house is ready. You need a place of your own."

"Oh, Ingrid, I couldn't. You put so much work into it," Anne said.

"No, really, I mean it. We did it for you."

Anne hugged Ingrid. "You're an angel."

CC joined in on the hug, cleared her throat and with a rough voice that was more of a whisper. "Annie, I'm so sorry. You know I love you."

"I know. I'm sorry, too." Anne said. "Wait a minute." She ran down the stairs.

CC stared at Ingrid. "I was hoping to make this my apartment," Ingrid said, "at least until I finished school."

CC hugged her. "This is very generous of you."

Anne came back, hugging three tapestry pillows. "Oh my couch will be perfect in here right across from the fireplace. This is fabulous." She put the pillows on the red chairs and sank down into one. "Ingrid, we have to go shopping, and you can help me bring my things over tomorrow. CC, if you can bear me for one more night?"

"Hush up, you're being silly," CC said.

They went downstairs and out onto the front porch. As CC locked the front door, Anne noticed lights on in the sweet shop next door. "Should be opening soon," Anne said. "I wonder what kind of store it will be. Did John tell you who bought the store?"

"I spoke to him a while back. He fell through the ceiling when he fell off a ladder so they fired him. He's on workman's comp."

"Oh? Probably better that way."

CC agreed.

Chapter Sixteen

The next morning, Anne got up early, eager to move her clothes to the new apartment. She had stayed up half the night, searching for items on eBay to complement her new abode. After loading up her Mercedes and CC's VW, they headed to the shop and parked in the back. Anne wandered around to the front of the store and that's when she saw a flash of periwinkle blue turning the corner heading down the street toward the store. "Buttersworth," she murmured, "Not again." She went into the shop, locking the door behind her. She waited and waited. Buttersworth never showed up. She couldn't be mistaken. That color was synonymous with her arch antique hunting nemesis and, though no relation to the syrup, always a sticky problem for Anne. Last time Anne had seen her, they'd had a battle royale right in the middle of Great-Aunt Sybil's Attic. No antique had been left standing. "I don't understand," Anne said, peeking out the window again.

"Understand what? And why is the door locked?" CC asked, opening the door and turning the *open* sign around. Anne's question was answered when they both stepped out onto the front porch and saw the sign being erected onto the top of the shop next door. In large bold, screaming periwinkle blue letters, it proclaimed *Buttersworth's*, and in smaller letters, it read *Sweet Boutique.*

"NO!!!!" Anne screamed. "Buttersworth!" The poor finches that had landed on the feeder fell onto the ground. A car alarm went off in the distance. Anne collapsed onto the steps of the front porch. CC sat next to her, her arm around her friend's shoulders.

Betsy Buttersworth came out the front door of the shop next door and waved to Anne.

Chapter Seventeen

"The Great Chicago Fire burned from Sunday, October 8, to early Tuesday, October 10, 1871. It killed up to 300 people and destroyed 3.3 square miles of Chicago, leaving more than 100,000 residents homeless," CC read out loud to Nick as they entered the exhibit hall devoted to the tragedy. They were at the Chicago History Museum just outside the city's prestigious Lincoln Park neighborhood.

After meeting Catherine, CC wanted to learn more about the fire and had invited Nick to join her. The first part of the exhibit detailed what had happened on those few days. "Nick, this is fascinating. I'm learning so much about the history of the fire," CC said as she studied a painting depicting hordes of residents fleeing the city. The display featured items found after the fire, including two silver watches fused together, melted marbles and various doll heads.

"Can you imagine the horror people must have felt?" CC asked.

"Unfortunately, I can. I've seen what fire can do," Nick said.

"Of course, Nick, I wasn't thinking." CC interlocked her arm around Nick, rubbing the scar marks on his upper arm.

"The Chicago Fire Academy where I trained is located on the original spot where the fire started—Mrs. O'Leary's barn."

"You know that's just a myth, right?" CC asked as they stepped in front of a panel that read Legend of the

Chicago Fire and Web of Memories. It had eyewitness accounts, newspaper clippings from the day, art and finally the legend of Mrs. O'Leary and her cow. Underneath the image was the cowbell allegedly worn by Daisy, the cow.

CC read, "According to one story, Catherine O'Leary admitted that she was in the barn when one of her cows kicked over a lantern. Another story states Mrs. O'Leary swears she was in bed when the fire started. Yet another story states that her son ran an illegal gambling ring in her barn and the fire was caused by drunken gamblers. After the fire, a few curiosity seekers claimed to have found broken pieces of the lantern when sneaking around her cottage, which had somehow survived the fire. Years later, a man came forward stating that as a boy he had found the lantern under some floorboards in the barn. He could not produce the lantern because he said it had been stolen as part of a cover-up. Editorials alleged that the Chicago fire department was more concerned with looking good and not taking blame. No real investigation was ever conducted. As for Mrs. O'Leary, after death threats to her and her family, she moved out of Chicago."

"Very interesting," Nick said. "Why are we here?"

"I told you about the lantern and Mrs. O'Leary's descendent. We gave her the lantern but something about it has bothered me," CC said.

"What's that? According to everything you read, it's probably not even the original lantern. This is all urban myth," Nick said.

"Patricia Rounder, fugitive, wanted for murder, comes to America, steals a car and comes to our antique store. Then she dies," CC said. "She was carrying a 1800s lantern. Catherine Henderson's address was in the GPS of the stolen car. And, then I find out that

Catherine Henderson is a descendent of Mrs. O'Leary. Don't you find that a bit coincidental?"

"So you think the lantern has something to do with Patricia's murder?" Nick asked.

"I'm not sure." CC paused. "When Anne gave her statement, she told the officers about the lantern and offered to submit it as evidence. They couldn't find any connection or anything unusual other than the fact that Patricia was carrying it when she died," CC said. "There's a lot about Patricia Rounder we don't know yet and that's why we're here today. She chose to spend the last few minutes of her life at Great-Aunt Sybil's Attic so we owe it to her to find out why."

Chapter Eighteen

CC tripped over a pile of boxes teetering on the edge of the stairs in the store. "Anne," she called up the stairs.

There was no response. "Anne," she called again. Still no response. She weaved past the boxes and headed upstairs to what was now Anne's small apartment. She knocked on the door. Still no answer. She opened the door to see the back of her friend sitting in the wingback chair. A large pair of headphones covered Anne's ears. She was bobbing her head along to some unheard beat. CC raised one of the ear cuffs. "Anne. I've been calling you for 10 minutes."

Anne removed the headphones. "I didn't hear you, CC. I was listening to Lily's album. She's really blown up. She's had three number one hits in a row. I didn't tell you but I emailed her to congratulate her and then she called me. We talked for almost an hour. She's working on her second album. She said that she felt bad she hadn't thanked us on the first album. She's going to put a special thanks to Anne and CC, the Spoon Sisters, and include a link to our blog. She's quite the toast of Nashville, and she's coming to Chicago."

"That's really great. She's a sweet girl, Anne," CC sighed. "But we're getting everything ready for the wedding. It's in a week." CC sat on the chair across from Anne. "What are all those boxes on the stairs? It's a fire hazard." Fire had been on CC's mind a lot lately after visiting the history museum.

"I found more linen. I've had them in storage locker Number 3. I stumbled across them when I went to get my Eastlake mirror for the bathroom. You haven't even said anything about what I've done with the place."

CC glanced around at the encroaching clutter. It was beginning to resemble Anne's old house on a smaller scale. Antique hatboxes piled up in the corner, the table next to the chair overflowing with books and a pile of laundry. "It's very cozy up here."

"You have to see this." Anne led CC into the bedroom. Sassy was lying on the bed and the kitten was sunbathing in the window. "Adam knocked out the old window and put in this garden window. It's the perfect venue for the cats. Don't you think? They love it. I'm thinking of hanging a bird feeder right outside it. Can you imagine?"

"This is all well and good but we should sort through what you found to see what else we need for the wedding."

"Oh, that sounds great. I can't remember what's in the boxes. They're all marked Irish lace." Anne tried to hide back her enthusiasm. She couldn't remember what was in the boxes. It had been so long since she had purchased them.

Anne and CC went downstairs, moving the boxes off the stairs into the store. Sassy and Sybil followed close behind, doing what they could to help by winding through Anne and CC's legs as they maneuvered the steep stairs.

"I'm locking up the store now," Ingrid said. "Sorry I can't stay to help you prepare for the wedding. I have a study group at the library."

"CC, you have to read Ingrid's paper," Anne said. "It's very good. You know it's on me, right?"

"Yes, I know. It's about a modern day heroine for her fiction class," CC emphasized the word *fiction*.

"It's based on Anne and her adventures." Ingrid gave them both a hug goodbye. Anne handed her the Mercedes keys.

"What are you doing?" CC asked.

"We're going to be here most of the night and I've got nowhere to go. I told Ingrid she could borrow my car."

"I don't know if it's right for an 18-year-old to be driving around in a $100,000 SUV."

$117,000," Anne whispered to herself.

"What?"

"Oh, nothing. It's just the library and then back to your house." Anne didn't tell CC that the library was downtown and so was the bar Ingrid was going to afterwards.

"Thanks, Anne. Bye." Ingrid flew out the door, closing it quickly behind her and locking it.

Anne pulled the packing tape off a box, opening it to reveal lace tablecloths. CC picked one up, unraveling it. "These are beautiful, Anne; where'd you find them?"

"That one is from Limerick, I think from about 1840. I believe it was made during the potato famine. Imagine some poor woman, trying to earn money to put food on her table, sewing this for a fancy house. And look at this one; I forgot I had it." Anne pulled out a tablecloth decorated with embroidered colorful flowers. "This is like the one that they turned into a coat for Cora on *Downton Abbey*. Remember we saw the exhibit at the Driehaus and the costume designer explained that they wanted to use authentic fabric."

"That does look exactly like her dress. These are really interesting pieces, Anne."

"Each one, or at least most of these, have the provenance. Some were sold as a lot at a downtown auction house. Help me carry this chest down." Anne grabbed one end of a cedar chest which she had parked at the landing. CC took the other end. They brought it down the narrow stairs, bumping the walls as they went.

"This is really old, Anne," CC said, staring at the chest.

"It's an Irish Queen Anne blanket chest. It was one of the items I found in Paris at the chateau estate sale."

"I thought we sold everything from that trip."

"Well, not everything." Anne didn't explain that she had kept the Limoges bee salt and pepper shakers or the French cast metal vitrine. Or the Lalique perfume bottle. Or the. . no sense listing more than that. It was all safe in one of her five storage lockers. "The original owner of the estate was a wholesaler who sold textiles. He had silks from China, cashmere from England, then this lace from Ireland."

CC stared at the inside of the chest. "It says 1740, Anne. This chest is from 1740. That lettering there is the Ogham symbol for cedar."

"What's Ogham?"

"It's an ancient Celtic language. Most of the symbols in the alphabet refer to trees."

"How do you know all this stuff?" Anne asked.

"I have a curious mind. I first saw Ogham when I attended a shipbuilding conference in Belfast. We toured the Harland & Wolff Titanic shipyard. It was really interesting. The RMS Celtic was launched from that yard in 1901, and that's where I remember seeing the Ogham lettering. It was on the ship." CC thought for a moment. She had seen it somewhere else recently. It came back to her. "I saw it on the lantern."

"What are you talking about?" Anne asked. "I thought the scrollwork on the sleeve around the bottom of the lantern was decorative. I do remember seeing an Ogham symbol on the lantern. We have to go take a look."

"Now?" Anne pictured her cozy apartment upstairs with her hot chocolate and sugar cookies. She had picked out a good book to read. She had started rereading all the *Anne of Green Gables* books. "Oh, CC, we have a lot of work ahead of us. I have plans for tonight."

"Anne, Patricia Rounder died in our store, carrying that lantern."

"Yes, CC, I know. I try to block that from my memory," Anne said. "She came to me for help and I couldn't help her."

"We're going to help her now, Anne," CC said.

They left the building, locking it behind them and went to CC's VW. A light drizzle started as they got on the highway. Anne's eBay's annoying pinging began. CC's head throbbed. "Anne, can you turn that down please?"

"I can't turn it too soft. I'm watching a set of Wedgewood gold china plates."

"Anne, you don't need anymore china."

"You can never have too many sets of china, and I might resell it."

CC sighed. Anne's logic sometimes left her speechless. CC turned the wipers to full speed as the drizzle changed to a steady downpour. The early summer corn danced to the beat of the rain. The VW's tires hydroplaned on the muddy washed-out road. Anne's face was glowing from her iPhone, and the pings were constant. CC strained her eyes to see though the windshield.

"We're here," CC said as she jerked the bus to a stop.

Anne checked her phone. "It's 9:30. It's kind of late to just show up. Don't you think we should call first?"

"I texted Catherine when we left the store. She never got back to me."

"Maybe that's because she doesn't want company." Anne had an uneasy feeling. Old farmhouses in the middle of nowhere on rainy nights were better left to cozy mysteries than real life. As they closed the car doors, the porch light turned on and the door opened. Catherine stepped onto the porch.

"You got my message," CC said as they ran up the front steps clutching their umbrellas over their heads.

"No, I didn't. I get very bad cell phone reception out here. I saw headlights coming up the drive. This late at night I was a bit concerned," the old lady said. "Come inside. I'll make us some tea." As Mrs. Henderson turned in the doorway, CC noticed the kitchen knife in her hand. Catherine followed CC's gaze down. "I was cleaning chickens for tomorrow's lunch. I must look a mess." She glanced down at her bloody apron. Catherine continued into the house. Anne followed, not watching her steps, instead keeping her gaze on her iPhone. She was in hot pursuit of 14-carat jadeite art deco earrings—for her—not the store. CC put her arm out, stopping Anne before she could cross the threshold. Anne looked up as Mrs. Henderson turned around. "Please, come in."

"We really didn't want to bother you this late at night. I'm so sorry we came out. We wanted to take another look at the lantern," CC said.

Mrs. Henderson walked back closer to the doorway. "Why do you want to see the lantern?"

"I've done some research, and I believe it could be a very valuable historic piece. I notice it wasn't hanging on the porch where you said you were going to put it," CC said.

"I did hang it on the porch but this morning it was gone. Sometimes things have legs around here. So many people coming and going. You can imagine, can't you?"

"Thank you. So sorry we bothered you. We better get back on the road before the storm gets worse," CC said.

Catherine stood uncomfortably close to CC. "I can't let you two go. Not in a downpour like this. Please come in. At least dry off while we wait for the rain to let up."

"Do you have anymore of that fresh-baked bread and honey? Or maybe some of those gingersnaps?" Anne asked.

"I'm sorry but we must go." CC pulled Anne by the arm toward the VW. She shoved Anne into the passenger side and slammed the door. She threw the bus in reverse, speeding backwards down the long, gravel driveway, stones flying out from her tires like a shotgun blast, until she reached the access road and turned around.

"What's got into you?" Anne exclaimed.

"She was holding a butcher knife."

"She said she was cleaning chickens for lunch. She runs a restaurant."

"Anne, the lantern is gone."

"She said somebody took it. I really think you're getting carried away," Anne said, turning to look at CC.

CC pulled over to the side of the road half into a ditch. "Anne, I can't see. We have to wait until the rain lets up."

"I knew this was a bad idea." Anne pictured her cozy living room with her cup of cocoa, her book and her Persians.

"Anne."

"Yes, CC."

"Patricia was stabbed to death."

Anne stared at CC.

"We have to get out of here," she said. CC put the bus in gear and slid on back to the road. A pair of headlights appeared coming towards them. The headlights fishtailed, coming into their lane.

"CC, look out," Anne screamed.

CC swerved, landing them into the drainage ditch to avoid the pick-up truck that sped past them. CC's heart was pounding; Anne clenched her arm. "We have to be careful. The road is slippery." CC put the bus in drive, she checked the rearview mirror to see the red taillights stop and turn around so the headlights were facing them. "We've got to go, Anne." CC put her foot to the pedals. The tires spun in the mud.

"Hurry, CC." Anne stared behind them as the headlights grew closer. The VW's tires churned and churned, spitting mud.

"We're just digging ourselves in deeper," CC said. "Get out."

Anne struggled with the door handle. CC reached over and pulled the door lock. Anne fell out of the car, landing into the ditch. CC ran around and dragged her out. Anne was clutching her large orange Prada bag. They struggled to climb out of the ditch but couldn't find a hold in the slippery mud. When they finally reached solid ground the truck slammed into the VW. Both vehicles slid down the road until they were stopped by a large billboard. The red taillights burned bright red and the truck spun back in reverse toward them.

CC grabbed Anne. They ran into the cornfield. The early summer stalks snapped as they ran down the rows. They could hear the truck engine whining, tires spinning and then the snapping of the corn behind them. CC grabbed Anne's arm, pulling her off to the right as the truck continued straight through the field. The husks scraped against their skin. Anne winced and moaned, huffing and puffing. Her large orange Prada bag flew behind her. They reached the end of the cornfield. Anne bent over, catching her breath. CC glanced around frantically for any glimpse of the headlights. The rain stopped. In the distance, they could see a fluorescent red glow that gave Anne a burst of energy. She grabbed CC. They ran across the open field, cross the two-lane highway. Anne stood in the parking lot, looking up at the glowing red "Hot Now" Krispy Kreme doughnut sign. A muddy pick-up truck flew into the parking lot. The sheriff who was sitting at the counter turned around to look at them.

"Saved by doughnuts," Anne said.

Chapter Nineteen

Anne accepted the free warm glazed doughnut and then ordered another. While she fished for her wallet, CC went over to talk to the sheriff. CC noticed his sidearm was a revolver, not the standard issue automatic 9 mm. The lines in his face served as markers for the trouble he had seen. "Sheriff, we need help," she said.

He ran a hand through his white crew cut. He sipped his coffee and set down his cup. He glanced CC over. She was drenched, caked in mud. "What've you been up to?"

"There was an accident, not really an accident. A pick-up truck ran into my VW van," CC said as Anne brought her a cup of coffee and her free doughnut.

"I need to see your driver's license."

"I left my purse inside my van."

"Where's your van?"

CC became flustered. "The van is stuck on the access road past that field. A pick-up truck slammed into it and chased us through the cornfield."

The sheriff looked over CC again and took another sip of his coffee. "Ma'am, you might want to sit down. You look like you're in shock."

CC raised her voice. "In shock. Yes, I'm in shock. We were chased through a cornfield in the middle of a rainstorm by a maniac trying to run us over."

"Did you get a look at the other vehicle?"

"No, but I know it was a pick-up truck."

"How do you know that?"

"It had rail lights above the cab. All I could see were the headlights and the rail lights on top of the cab. It was a big pickup truck by the height of the top lights."

"Not much to go on." He finished his coffee, put a single on the table and stood up.

"Aren't you going to call somebody? Do something?" CC asked.

"I'm going to call you a paramedic to make sure you two are okay."

"We're not hurt. We're fine but. . ."

"I'm off duty now. I was heading home. This isn't my jurisdiction. It's across county lines. I'm going to call the Hampshire police. They'll send a uniform out to help you." He grabbed his coat from the back of the chair before walking out.

CC sat next to Anne at the counter and sipped her coffee. Her hands shook from the cold and from anger. She watched him walk to his cruiser. She waited for him to call on his radio. Instead he pulled out his cell phone. She couldn't make out what he said. She had tried in journalism school to learn lip reading but he was too far away. He got in his cruiser and took off. CC looked over at Anne, who appeared to be on her third glazed doughnut. Anne's hair was caked with mud, her clothes just as muddy as CC's. "Anne, we do look bizarre."

Anne gazed around the restaurant which was empty. "It's almost midnight in the boondocks. What do you care? What's going on with the sheriff? Why didn't he make a report?"

"He said it wasn't his jurisdiction. He was going to send someone."

Anne didn't say anything, instead licking the warm sugar from her fingers. She ate when she was upset. At least that's what she told herself.

A short while later, a young Hampshire police office walked into Krispy Kreme. Anne and CC told him their story and he drove them to the access road where the VW was supposed to be. But it wasn't.

Chapter Twenty

By the time the Uber driver dropped the Spoon Sisters off at CC's, the sun was coming up. Anne could see the long, tall silhouette of Nigel illuminated on the front porch. It had taken hours for them to fill out the stolen vehicle report and tell their story. Anne fell into safety, into Nigel's arms. He carried her in, followed by CC.

"Nigel, thank you for coming," CC said. They sat at the dining room table, Bandit dancing at their feet.

Anne had explained to him via text what had happened. He stared back and forth at both of them. "I must look a mess," Anne said.

"Why don't the two of you go get tidied up and changed? I'll make us some breakfast and then we'll talk," Nigel said.

Anne came back first wearing a pink velvet bathrobe, dabbing at her hair with a towel. CC followed shortly after in jeans and a t-shirt. Nigel was standing at the stove wearing CC's gingham apron. He was flipping pancakes. He glanced over his shoulder at Anne and smiled. He fixed a plate for the three of them and sat down. Bandit sat down next to Nigel. He had learned the English loved dogs. Nigel always reinforced that with a handful of scraps under the table. "I've talked to the Hampshire police," Nigel said. "No luck with the VW so far. They searched the cornfield and were able to get an approximation of the size and weight of the truck from the path laid down through the corn. CC, Anne told me after you reached the Krispy Kreme, you spoke with a sheriff."

"Yes, he wasn't very helpful."

"Jurisdiction or not, he should have stayed to make sure you were safe and followed through. I couldn't find any report from the Kane County sheriff's department."

"He never gave me his name, and I didn't see his name tag," CC said.

"I'll follow up with the Hampshire police," Nigel said. "What were you two doing out there that late at night in a rainstorm?"

"It's a long story, Nigel. It started when I—I mean we—were getting Irish linen ready for the wedding," Anne said.

"What wedding is that?"

"I didn't tell you. We've become wedding planners. Not really wedding planners but we're renting tablecloths and vases for a friend of ours who is a wedding planner out at the Sanfillipo estate in Barrington."

"That's nice, Anne, but let's get back to the story," Nigel said.

"The mansion is supposed to be beautiful; I've never been because it's closed unless you go with a group. Why don't you come? You can help."

"That sounds aces. Let's get back to last night," he repeated.

"On my cedar blanket chest, CC noticed a symbol."

"It's Ogham," CC interrupted.

"Ogham. Many headstones in England and Ireland have Ogham symbols," Nigel said.

"And then CC remembered seeing an Ogham symbol on the lantern that we gave Mrs. Henderson. We wanted to go out and take a closer look but the lantern had been stolen off her porch."

"You two lady detectives are at a loose end, aren't you?"

"Excuse me," CC said in an indignant voice.

"That means you have too much spare time on your hands."

"What do you mean too much spare time? We've got the store. We've got the blog. We just held an estate sale."

"No, I didn't mean that literally. What I meant was that things are getting as black as Newgate's knocker."

"What does that mean?" CC asked.

"Nigel slips into British slang when he gets upset," Anne whispered.

"Newgate is an infamous prison so its doorknocker means trouble, and that's where you two are headed. If you want to learn more about Ogham, our department is handling security at the Irish festival at Gaelic Park this weekend. I was going to ask Anne if she wanted to come out. Maybe you should come, too, CC. Take your mind off your worries and you can learn more about Ogham, history and such."

"I think we could use a break. What do you say, Anne?" CC asked.

"I'll invite Ingrid, Adam and Nick. We can triple date."

Nigel smiled. "All righty, it's a triple date then. We'll meet up on Saturday and then Bob's your uncle."

Chapter Twenty-One

Large party tents dotted the two long Irish football fields at Chicago's Gaelic Park. Inside one tent were the incredible Irish dancers, kicking their heels, arms held firmly at their sides. On the sidelines, Anne tried to dance along, spilling Guinness all over. Adam and Nick walked up behind her, carrying more glasses of Guinness. Nick yelled to be heard over the music, "CC, we have a table over in the corner. Let's go sit down."

Nick and Adam, CC and Anne sat at a small table by the side of the stage. Anne yelled, "Where's Ingrid?"

Adam nodded at the stage. The Irish dancers were bringing up audience members for a dance lesson. Ingrid was wearing a green and gold Celtic dance dress. Her beautiful long blonde hair was braided. One of the dancers stood in front of her, showing her moves. Ingrid picked it up immediately. She turned in the chorus line, with the rest of the volunteers and kicked her long legs. Anne stood up and cheered, jumping along. One of the dancers grabbed Anne, pulling her onto the stage. CC laughed, shaking her head *no*. The music pounded away. Anne watched Ingrid and tried to kick, one of her wedge Clarks flew into the crowd. She gasped and ran after it.

After Ingrid came off stage, Anne said, "Let's go get some food, maybe look at the crafts."

They wandered along the craft area, pausing to look at displays of Irish sweaters, dance costumes, jewelry. CC stopped at a vendor selling food. "This is coddle, isn't it?"

The cheery red-haired woman explained, "Yes, it's layers of sliced pork sausage, bacon, fattyback bacon, sliced potatoes and onions."

"It looks delicious," CC said, sniffing the aroma.

Anne popped up behind her. "Yes, it does look delicious. What are we eating?" She was wearing a large "Kiss me, I'm Irish" button and an even larger shamrock headpiece.

"It's coddle. It's filled with homemade sausage and onions."

"I'm in," Anne said.

They both bought a little bowl and nibbled as they walked. "Oh, what's that?" Anne stopped at another booth.

CC sniffed and peeked closer. "Cottage pie. It's beef and vegetables mixed with a delicate beef sauce topped with mashed potatoes. Sort of like shepherd's pie but without the minced lamb."

"I'm in," Anne said. They nibbled some more.

When they reached the final booth, they found dessert. "Anne, this is really quite good. I had it when I was in Belfast. It's called gur cake. Gur is what they call young lads up to no good, the phrase *go on the gur*, means to skip school, and that's where the cake got its name because it's made from leftover stale bread. It's one of the cheapest things to buy from the baker so young lads on the gur would buy pieces of gur cake to fuel their school skipping activities. It's moistened butter cake crumbs mixed with fruit and sugar and spread between two sheets of pastry."

"I'm in," Anne said, waving cash in the air.

The young girl serving the gur cake, reached over with two plates of cake for CC. CC noticed a Celtic gold cross hanging from her neck. There was an Ogham symbol in the middle of the cross. "Excuse me, miss, your cross is beautiful."

The young woman grabbed it and pulled it back to her chest. "Thank you. Thank you, ma'am."

"That symbol on the cross; what does it mean?" CC asked.

The young girl did the sign of the cross and then kissed it. She tucked it back into her blouse. "That symbol is for oak tree. My grandmother passed last month and we buried her under an oak tree at Mount Olive."

"Oh."

"It's an old Irish custom. It makes it easier for the angels to find her if she's buried by a tree. And then we engrave that tree on our cross to help guide the angels to the right tree."

"What a great way to remember her," CC said.

"Yes, she was a lovely woman. I miss her everyday," the young girl said.

CC paid for the cake. She and Anne walked over to the open field. "What are they doing?" Anne asked, staring out at the field. Nigel was flinging his arms about with a stick, trying to drive a ball down the field, Adam and Nick chasing behind.

"They're hurling, Anne; they're hurling," CC said. "It's the oldest field game in Europe. It goes back thousands of years."

They watched as Nigel leaped over fallen hurlers like a giant grasshopper. He flew past Anne and tipped his hurler's cap towards her. He was wearing the green and gold of the South Side Irish. CC and Anne giggled at the sight. They sat on the grass with the other spectators. When the match was over, Nigel came over and sat down next to Anne who leaned against his elbow. "You are quite the sportsman," Anne said.

"If you think my hurling is good, you should see my cricket," Nigel said.

"Where'd you get the uniform?" Anne asked.

"All the officers who volunteered to help out today received a swag bag. They asked us if we wanted to play in some of the games so here we are then. How's the triple date going?"

"CC and Ingrid seem to be doing fine." They looked over at Ingrid who was kissing Adam on the sidelines.

Then they looked at CC and Nick who were laughing as they shared the rest of the gur cake.

"But there hasn't been much time for you and me, has there?" Nigel asked, looking over at Anne. Her soft blonde hair luminescent in the sunlight, her eyes wide and sparkling blue. Her yellow polka dot sundress was slipping off her shoulder. Nigel righted it. Anne smiled. She reached over and kissed him.

Nigel wrapped his bony arms around her, kissing her gently on the lips, pressing his bony chest against her. Anne loved the way Nigel felt against her. She closed her eyes and let the moment take her away. And then a fight broke out between the opposing teams. Nigel jumped up. "I'm sorry, Anne, I have to go." He hopped off onto the field.

Anne fell back on her elbows and hmmphed. She could still taste him on her lips. CC plopped down next to Anne. "What's wrong, Annie?"

"Nigel's on the clock."

"I saw you two kissing. Is it getting serious?"

"I think I've had too much to drink," Anne said.

"Nick and Adam had to leave. Ingrid went with them. Something at the firehouse," CC said.

"That's okay. We might as well get going. It looks like Nigel will be busy for a while."

Anne got up and wobbled.

"Whoa, whoa. I think you did have a little too much to drink." CC put her arm on her friend to steady her.

"Must have been those Irish whiskey samples."

"We better get you home. We'll call Nigel later and let him know," CC said.

Anne smiled, and said, "Yes, Nigel. We'll call him." Anne took off her wedge heels, dangling them from her hand.

CC took Anne by the arm and walked her through the crowd. Strains of the Irish fiddles followed them. They walked behind the tents into the woods. "Why are we going through here?" Anne asked.

"The parking lot is on the other side. It's faster than going around the whole park," CC said.

"I have to sit for a moment. I'm getting dizzy."

CC looked around and found a tree stump. Anne sat down and looked up at the sky. "Look, CC, an oak tree. The angels can find us."

"What?" CC asked. "Oh, yeah, the cross, that's right."

"I think Nigel could make me happy. I could make a life with him, a family."

CC sat down on the stump next to Anne. "Nigel's a wonderful man. Let's talk about this later. Are you okay to stand now? It's getting dark. We better get going." CC helped Anne up.

"Which way, CC?"

CC looked around. "It's. . .it's. I think it's that way." She pointed ahead. They walked.

"What was that?" Anne asked.

"What?" CC said. Then she heard the noise. "Quiet."

They started walking again. CC stopped. "Listen."

"I don't know what you're talking about, CC."

"Shh, Anne, quiet," CC whispered.

Anne listened carefully. Her head pounded. She rubbed her temple and then she heard it: crackling, sticks, snapping under foot. "Someone's coming," CC said. "Let's go, Anne."

They hurried their pace, winding their way through the trees. The footsteps followed them. "CC, which way? Where's the car?" Anne asked in a panicked tone. Anne dropped her shoes and came to a dead stop. "Wait, my shoe."

"Just leave it, Anne." CC pulled her along.

"Which way?" Anne repeated.

"I don't know, Anne. I'm turned around."

The footsteps quickened. CC took Anne's hand and ran. The shadows of the trees grew longer and the trail disappeared. CC pulled Anne into a hollowed out tree and put her hand over Anne's mouth. "I can't breathe, CC," she muffled.

"Quiet."

The footsteps came, stopped in front of the tree. They could hear a man's breathing, low and gnarled. They heard a metal clink. CC peeked out to see the small flame of a lighter and then the red glow of a cigarette. She couldn't make out the man on the other end of it. He took several puffs and then threw it to the ground stamping it out. He then disappeared into the darkness.

Anne mumbled, "CC, I can't breathe."

"Sorry, Anne." She pulled her hand off Anne's mouth.

"Did you see who that was?"

"No, Anne, I couldn't make out his face." They climbed out of the hollow. CC turned on her iPhone and pointed the light at the ground. She walked along in a serpentine trail searching until she found it, the cigarette he had thrown. She picked it up and smelled it.

"What are you doing?"

"I know this scent. Give me a second." CC paused. "I've smoked this."

"What do you mean? I thought you quit smoking."

"This is years ago when I was in Belfast back when I was smoking. It was 2011. This is a P. J. Carroll and Company, the largest tobacco manufacturer in Ireland," CC said. "I know this smell. It's sweeter than their other cigarettes. It's sweet Afton. Launched in 1919, they were named after a poem by Robert Burns. His sister Agnes was buried in a graveyard across from the old Carroll factory on Church Street in Dundalk. I remember visiting that graveyard."

"We're at Irish Fest. Of course there's Irish tobacco," Anne said.

"Yeah, Anne, but these cigarettes were discontinued in 2011."

Chapter Twenty-Two

CC balanced the basket of apples while she reached up to pick another from her overflowing tree. Bandit danced around her feet, chasing bumblebees, occasionally shaking his head. "Silly, Boo," CC said, watching him spit out one particularly large bee. He snapped at it again and then bit down.

She picked a lemon from her potted lemon tree. "Come on, Boo, let's get this chutney ready for our picnic." She opened the sliding door into her sunroom. Bandit flew in first. He sniffed the floor and let out a low growl. Then he took off into the rest of the house, sniffing corners, letting out low growls. "What's wrong, Boo? Do you miss Sassy and Sybil?"

Bandit turned around at the sound of CC's voice, tilting his head, giving her an "as if" look. CC went into the kitchen. Bandit lay protectively near her feet. "Let's start by preparing the apples," she said. She peeled, cored and chopped two pounds of tart apples into half inch pieces. She boiled vinegar and sugar in a large cast iron saucepan. Two cups apple cider vinegar, two cups of sugar, went in. She stirred until the sugar dissolved. She reduced the heat while it simmered. Bandit walked up behind her and sat at attention. CC caught a glimpse of that beautiful Aussie grin. She handed him a piece of tart apple. He took it, shook his head but ate it anyway. She placed the apples in a large bowl, adding three tablespoons fresh lemon juice. She opened her spice rack and grabbed dried crushed red peppers she had grown in her garden. For a second she looked at the jar that said ghost pepper but then thought better of it, even though she knew Nick would appreciate the zing it would give the chutney. She combined garlic, ginger, salt, red pepper in her processor and blended it. She added apple, garlic, raisins and mustard seed to the vinegar. She simmered it until the apples were tender. After a while, she placed it in a bowl to cool. Bandit lay in the corner of the kitchen, watching intently. In the past couple weeks, he had not left her side. It wasn't so unusual for her Aussie but something was different, something was bothering him. CC knelt down next to Bandit. She rubbed his ears and rewarded him with a kiss. "Bandit, I'm worried about you. You haven't been yourself. I was just kidding about Sassy and Sybil. You seem very stressed out. We're going for a nice walk in a little bit. Let me write my blog and then we'll go."

Bandit agreed with a kiss. CC gathered the soda bread she had made early that morning and the selection of Kerrygold cheeses she had sliced. She put everything in a picnic basket. "Oh, I almost forgot." She ran downstairs and selected a nice vintage of her cherry wine. "Almost ready, Boo."

She sat down at the dining room table and opened her laptop. Bandit walked over to the table, circled several times and then lay down at CC's feet, giving out one last low growl. "Dear Friends," she typed. "Yesterday we went to Irish Fest in Gaelic Park. Even though I've lived here for many years, it was my first time at this festival. Anne and I enjoyed several specialties, and I was able to convince the chef to give me his recipe for gur cake. He said it would be okay if I shared it with you." She added the recipe and a picture of the cake to the blog.

"I've added a picture of our dear friend, Detective Nigel Towers, in his hurling uniform. And Ingrid in her Irish dance costume. I've also added several images of some of the request items we found recently. Anne and I continue to handpick linens for an upcoming wedding. We have a new collection at the store of modern Hummels that were left over from the estate sale we ran. By the way, thank you to all who were able to attend.

"Mary Ann will be in the store, repairing china on Saturday if you need to stop by. And, don't forget next month we're having a book signing. If you've not had the opportunity to read Ginger Clark's series, they are truly fabulous. She writes cozy mysteries about the perilous world of antique hunting. Antique hunting. What an imagination. And, I don't want to brag but Anne and I may have provided the inspiration. At least, Anne believes she is one of the main characters.

"Great-Aunt Sybil's Attic is doing a booming business. We're so blessed. On a sadder note, my beloved 1968 VW microbus has yet to be located. Thank you all for your well wishes on that and for passing on the word. For today, Bandit and I are headed to the Glen Ellyn community garden. I will be posting some new images. The early tomatoes and cucumbers are doing quite well. Ripe for the picking. As always, thank you for being a part of our lives. You are dear friends. Your dear friend, CC."

CC grabbed her picnic basket, clipped on Bandit's leash. As she headed out the front door, Bandit pulled the leash out of her hands and ran to the back door. "Bandit, this way. We're going this way." Bandit stood still, standing at the door, growling. CC knelt down and whispered in his ear. "Boo, I'm worried about you. Let's go for a walk. You need to burn off some energy." CC peeked out the back door with an uneasy gaze. She shook it off.

They headed down the Prairie Path, their favorite haunt. The meadows were awash with color from summer sage, forget-me-nots, coneflowers, purple foxglove and yellow tickseed. Lavender lined the gravel path. CC stopped at a milkweed plant where she watched the monarchs preparing their family tree. Bandit charged at a woman speed walking with her headphones on, being pulled along by a longhaired corgi. Bandit was outraged. The corgi gave Bandit the stink-eye. Bandit dug his heels in, doing his best Fred Flintstone running in place impersonation. CC scolded him. "Really, Bandit, after having you certified as a therapy dog? Is that very therapeutic? Barking at that ugly little dog?"

Bandit ignored CC, giving one last woof at the retreating corgi. They continued down the path that led to the community garden plot which was lined with rows and rows of neatly planted crops. Several families were out tending their sections. A cute little girl, no more than six, in a sundress and floppy garden hat held a small copper watering can. She was very busy giving her sunflowers a drink. The little girl saw Bandit, ran up to him and hugged him. "Bandit," she giggled.

He wiggled his tailless butt and kissed her face uncontrollably. She giggled. The little girl's mom waved from her garden section. "Hi, Lisa. Your name's Lisa, right?" CC asked.

"Yes, Ms. Muller."

"I see your sunflowers are doing quite well."

"Aren't they beautiful? My mom said I could cut one and put it next to my bed."

"By the way, Lisa, did you know that sunflowers in many cultures were gathered for their natural source of fat. The seeds could be ground up and mixed with flour to make bread. About 5,000 years ago people began to farm them in Mexico and parts of North America. It was one of the first crops even before corn. The Cherokee Native Americans farmed sunflowers. It was an important part of their diet. Other parts of the plants were used for medical remedies like snakebites," CC said.

"Ms. Muller, I just think they're pretty."

"Yes, so do I, Lisa."

Lisa gave CC a hug and one last pat to Bandit. She ran back to her gardening. CC saw Nick, picking tomatoes. She went over to him, gave him a kiss. "I'm all sweaty," he said, taking his t-shirt off and wiping his face with it. His face glistened as sweat dripped down the ripples on his stomach.

CC blushed. "Hey, Nick why don't you take a break? I packed us some lunch. Let's sit under the oak tree. You're getting a bit red, you need to get out of the sun."

They walked over and sat under the tree. Bandit lay down across CC's feet. "What's wrong with Bandit?"

"He won't leave my side. He's been really tense the past couple weeks. Since." CC stopped and thought for a moment. "Since that night in Hampshire and my VW." Bandit turned his head around, looked up at CC. She could see the worry in his eyes. It made her worry.

"CC, I would feel a lot better if you'd stay with me for a while," Nick said.

"I'm fine. I have Ingrid and Bandit. Unless you're asking me to move in," she said with a smirk as Nick opened the bottle of wine.

Nick cleared his throat, stuttered out, "I meant . . ."

"No, I'm kidding. Look at you," CC interrupted. "I'm fine. Really, I'm fine." She laid out the chutney and cheeses. They laughed and shared their lunch. CC leaned up against the oak, staring up through its long strong branches. It was one of the oldest trees in Glen Ellyn. She thought back to the live oaks dripping with kudzu moss in her backyard in Louisiana where she had grown up. Climbing up its strong branches, hiding from the hot Louisiana sun in its cool arms, reading her history books. Reading about Amelia Earhart, Eleanor Roosevelt and her favorite, Nellie Blye, the intrepid journalist. The woman who inspired her to be a journalist. She whispered, "The angels in the oak tree."

"What was that?" Nick asked.

"Nothing," CC replied.

Chapter Twenty-Three

"Like this." Betsy Buttersworth waved her arms around the long table set up in the great hall of the Sanfillipo estate.

Anne stopped in her tracks, dropping the bin full of Irish linen, landing on her toes. CC pushed into her, almost sending her tumbling onto the floor. "Buttersworth," Anne's voice echoed throughout the great hall. She didn't know why her nemesis was here and why she was wearing a chef's apron and toque.

"Hillstrom," Buttersworth's reply came. She turned her eyes onto the Spoon Sisters. Anne could read *Buttersworth's Sweet Boutique* on the frilly white apron covering her long-time antique hunting foe.

"What's she doing here?" Anne muttered to CC.

CC stepped the few feet between them. "Hi, Betsy, we weren't expecting to see you here."

"Oh, Abby adores my truffles. She stopped in when she was leaving your store and asked me to cater a sweet table. So here I am." Betsy held her arms out.

"Why are you wearing a chef's hat?" Anne asked.

She pointed to the logo on the hat. "It's my store. Have you met Adelbert? He's my confectioner. He's from Belgium," Betsy said. She introduced them to a 30ish young man with flowing dark hair and pronounced features.

At any other point in her life, Anne would have been ecstatic to meet a Belgium confectioner but his association with Buttersworth ruined the flavor. She simply nodded.

"We have to stop in your store," CC said.

*Over my dead body*, Anne thought. She had avoided the sweet shop for two months even while continuously smelling the delicious melted chocolate. She wasn't going to start now. "CC, we have to put these linens out," Anne said.

"Abby mentioned you were bringing your castoffs here," Buttersworth said.

"Castoffs? Some of these linens are hundreds of years old," Anne said. "They're lucky we were able to rescue them."

"If that's what you call it," Betsy said. Then she giggled as Adelbert pinched her bottom as he walked out of the room.

Anne rolled her eyes.

"Toodoolooo, I have to fix the sweet table," Betsy said, turning her back to them again.

Anne sighed. "You know she opened that store next to us just to aggravate me," she whispered to CC.

"She's had a hard time. She's been lonely since you stole Nigel from her," CC said.

"Let's get this straight. She stole Nigel from me first, and Nigel left her."

"Either way, you and Nigel aren't really dating, are you?"

"We're taking it slow," Anne hissed through gritted teeth. She opened the box and pulled out the linens. She arranged them on the tables. CC followed behind her adding small crystal vases filled with Irish heather and fresh daisies to each place setting. When they were done, they stood back and surveyed the room.

"It's beautiful," CC said, snapping a photo with her iPhone to post on the blog.

Anne agreed. Abby came in, surveyed the room. "This is marvelous, Anne and CC. These linens are perfect. I hope you will stay and enjoy the reception."

Anne's enthusiasm grew. The reception included an open house. She'd be able to tour the estate, which was usually only open to tour groups and charities. While CC put the finishing touches on the tables, Anne stepped into the etched glass entryway that led into the Carousel Building, which held the Eden Palais carousel. She marveled at its amazing life-sized carved horses and its art glass butterflies. She stopped to admire the carousel and climbed on top of one of the hand-carved Hubner horses. She hummed to herself, picturing herself a character out of *Downton Abbey* in her silk morning frock, her lady's maid at her side. She took out her iPhone and snapped several selfies on the horse and then she sat at the Gavioli band organ and took several more. It was adorned with two large gold-leafed angel faces and a peacock with lighted feathers. She wondered if this would fit in her new house. Maybe in the first set of plans or the second, but by the time she reached the seventh redesign it would be a tight fit. Maybe she could build one on a smaller scale.

"Anne, what are you doing in here?" CC hissed from outside the doorway.

"Isn't this amazing?" Anne dragged her friend into the room.

"You know, Anne, the carousel platform runs on three tracks, three steam engines originally drove the platform," CC said. "The steam engines were restored but now the carousel is run by electricity."

"That's good, CC." Since she had moved out, Anne found she had more tolerance for CC's history lessons.

"Oh, here you are." Abby came into the room. "The wedding guests are on their way. You might want to come into the hall. I thought you would want to see their reactions when they see the tables."

They went back into the hallway and stood in a corner watching the guests file in. CC recognized a lot of them from amongst Chicago's elite: there were a few congressmen, a senator and Wayne Muscarello, a curator at the Field Museum. "Anne, Wayne's here."

Anne pulled her attention away from Betsy, who was nibbling a chocolate from the tips of her chocolatier's fingers. Anne thought Betsy had gained a few pounds since Nigel had left her. She saw Wayne. "I'll have to say hello to him," Anne said. "He's almost finished cataloguing Aunt Sybil's collection." Her Great-Aunt had left the family's collection of Viking swords and jewelry to the Field Museum as part of its permanent collection.

"Hi, CC, Anne." Wayne came over to them. "What an unexpected pleasure. It's nice to see you here."

"It's nice to see you, too. We're helping Abby with the table decorations from our antique store," CC said.

"Have you ever been to the Sanfillipo estate before?" Wayne asked.

"No, it's our first time," CC said.

"I've been here several times. I appraised their steam engine collection for the insurance company. They have the original Long John steam fire engine from 1858. It was put in service at the corner of Adams and Franklin streets," Wayne said.

"I'd love to see it," CC said.

As Wayne and CC droned on about the wonders of steam engines, Anne pictured lunching with the board members at the world-renowned Field Museum or perhaps here at the Sanfillipo estate. She would wear her gold tea dress, the one she'd bought in Paris. She'd have to remember to find matching shoes before the lunch.

"It was also used in the great Chicago fire," Wayne said.

"Do you think they'd let us look at it?" CC asked.

"It's closed for private tours but I can ask," Wayne said. He went and spoke to someone. When he came back, he said, "We have a few minutes before the reception starts."

CC and he slipped away to an outbuilding. Inside was a large horse-drawn wagon with a steam engine on the back. "The Chicago Fire Department kept a man with the wagon 24 hours a day to keep the fire stoked so it was always ready," Wayne said. "When they purchased the wagon, it stirred a lot of public outcry. The public didn't accept it at first because hand pumps were still more efficient, but the city knew that steam engines were the future. To add to the controversy, the fire marshal and some other city officials had an interest in the company that manufactured the steam engine wagon."

"Typical Chicago politics," CC said. She walked around admiring its steel frame. She ran a hand along the large wagon wheels. "What a fine piece of machinery. I can't believe it survived the fire," she said.

"The fire department was criticized for its slow response to the fire and its inability to contain it. A lot of the equipment never made it close to the burn zone," Wayne said. "They were diverted to Chicago's one percenters like Marshall Field and Potter Palmer to evacuate their merchandise. Even though Field's store burned down, the fire department saved his inventory so he was able to reopen less than a week after the fire, while the rest of the city burned to the ground and hundreds of thousands were left homeless. Another part of the whole Chicago fire myth."

CC noticed the back of the wagon, which had a plaque that read, "Engine No. 51." Under those letters, she saw stick symbols and the initials DJS. "Wayne, is this Ogham?"

"I'm very impressed. Not too many people are familiar with that language."

"I've read a little bit about it." She took a photo of the symbols with her iPhone.

"We have some early scrolls of Ogham at the Museum. Some of them date back to the Druids. It's a derivative of Phoenician, which was an alphabet of 22 letters carried around the world by wandering traders. It is a simplified form of hieroglyphics."

"I didn't know." CC admired Wayne's extensive knowledge of history. It rivaled her own. "I'll have to make time to come to the museum."

"A lot of the most valuable writings are locked in the vault in my office. You're always welcome," Wayne said. "Ogham was originally meant as a secretive code script. It was not used for general writing. It appears primarily on tombstones and boundary markers. According to legend, the scribes cast spells depending on the order of the letters. On gravestones they promised resurrection and travel between the worlds."

CC felt a chill. She took note of the Ogham symbol for an elm. "The angels are in the elms?"

"Yes, that Ogham symbol is for the elm tree. Seven firemen burned to death while evacuating Field's house on Elm Street."

"So the angels took their souls on Elm Street," she said. "Do you know whose initials these are? DJS?"

"That's for Dennis J. Swenie, first paid chief engineer of the Chicago fire department," Wayne said. "He was responsible for detouring many of the fire trucks to help his rich supporters like Field."

Chapter Twenty-Four

Nick balanced the picnic basket and blanket outside the festival gate while CC handed their tickets to the attendant at Ravinia Park. "You know, Nick, Ravinia was originally an amusement park when it opened in 1904," CC said as they searched for a spot on the lawn. "The theater is the only building on the grounds that is part of the original construction. It's the oldest outdoor music festival in North America."

Nick spread the blanket on the spot CC had selected. It was within viewing distance of the stage. Her friend, a former journalist colleague but now public relations director at Ravinia, had offered her main stage seating but she preferred the intimacy of sitting on the lawn. Nick took her hand and helped her down. He leaned back on his elbows, stretching out his legs. CC stole glimpses of him as she opened her vintage 1960s woven picnic basket. She reached in and grabbed a container. She fed him a spoonful of her shrimp and watermelon salad.

"Mmm, that's really good," Nick said.

"It's really easy. I based it on a dish I had at Buca di Beppo. It's shrimp with feta and watermelon garnished with a lemon dressing." CC pulled out a bottle of wine and a container of olives. She filled two glasses, handed one to Nick. He took a sip.

As the sun went down, the lawn filled up with blankets and chairs. They could hear the chatter of voices, the clinking of glasses. Stage lights came on.

Over the loudspeakers, there was an announcement, "Ladies and gentlemen, Lily Riddle."

CC clapped loudly. "This is her, Nick, the singer I told you about from Nashville who Anne and I discovered." CC pulled out Anne's mother-of-pearl opera glasses and viewed the stage. She could see Lily clad in a white lace dress and brown cowboy boots, holding her grandfather's Martin guitar. She walked up to the microphone and said, "This one's called *Young Hearts*."

Peering through the glasses, CC panned to Lily's right. She pulled the glasses away quickly and rubbed her eyes. She peered through them again and there was Brent, her Nashville fling, wearing only a leather vest over his bare chest with tight, faded jeans, his hair pulled back in a man bun. She put the glasses down and turned to Nick.

"Something wrong?" he asked.

CC smiled and said, "No." She gulped her wine and refilled her glass. She squirmed uncomfortably on the blanket. For the rest of the show, CC avoided looking at Brent, enjoying Lily Riddle's music. After the encore, CC stood up and helped Nick fold the blanket. "I'd like to go backstage and say hi to Lily," CC said.

"Sure," Nick said, taking the picnic basket from her. He followed her down the hill through the pavilion back to the side of the stage where a security guard was standing. CC flashed her press pass, and he waved them through.

Lily stood in the hallway talking to some fans. She saw CC and broke through the crowd. "CC, it's good to see you again," she said.

"This is my friend, Nick."

Lily looked Nick up and down, gave him a smile and shook his hand. "Thanks for coming."

"I enjoyed the show," he said.

As they talked, Brent came over wiping his face and chest with a towel. CC turned bright red. Brent tried to kiss CC on the cheek but she turned away. "Nick, this is Lily's guitar player, Brent," CC said.

"Guitar player?" Brent asked her, giving her a sly smile.

Nick nodded a greeting.

"We're going out for drinks. Do you want to come with us?" Lily asked. "We're going to Alice's Lounge. One of the roadies is from Chicago. She said it's a really great karaoke bar. We'll get our drank and our Hank on."

CC looked at Nick and asked, "Can we go?"

A short while later, Nick squeezed into a parking space near the north side bar. CC stared skeptically up at the small sign over the door. They entered a dark musty narrow bar. The oak bar top was stained with years of Pabst Blue Ribbon, whiskey sours and faded dreams of a Cubs World Series pennant. A pool table stood in one corner; in the opposite corner was a small stage where an elderly woman was blasting out, "Girls Just Want to Have Fun."

Nick and CC joined Lily and her friends at the high-top table. Lily brought over a pitcher of kamikazes. Everyone did a shot. "All right, CC, let's go." Lily grabbed her arm and pulled her up toward the stage without giving CC a chance to say no. Lily checked the song list, clicked a song on the iPad. The strains of "Family Tradition" by Hank Williams, Jr., started. As they belted out the song, Brent walked over and sat down next to Nick. He already had his fair share of kamikazes and was in a talkative mood.

"So, you and CC, uh?" he asked.

Nick didn't answer. He sipped his longneck Budweiser.

"So, is it serious?" Brent slurred his words.

Nick put his bottle down. "What are you trying to ask me?"

Brent took another shot. "I'm saying are you two serious? Exclusive?"

"I think you better slow down on those shots," Nick said.

CC reached behind Lily and grabbed the song list iPad. She was about to hit number 21, a John Hiatt song, when she heard bottles crashing. She looked out into the crowd and saw Nick standing over Brent, table overturned. She ran down to him. "We're leaving," Nick said.

CC stepped over Brent and grabbed Nick's hand. They went out onto Belmont Avenue. "What happened in there?" CC asked.

"He was asking the wrong questions," Nick said.

"Oh." She reached up and kissed Nick hard on the lips. Nick lifted her off the ground, returning her kiss.

Chapter Twenty-Five

"Anne, this is going to be a really tough case," Jon Berman said, staring at Anne from across his mahogany desk.

Anne looked around his law office, bookcases filled to the ceiling with books and journals. Behind him, a floor to ceiling window looking out onto Chicago's LaSalle Street, known as Attorney Row. "I don't understand. The house was there for over a hundred years. It's not my fault that they built it on a haunted Indian burial ground."

Berman smiled. "The stay doesn't state 'haunted,' but nevertheless the law at that time permitted the building. The Preservation Act hadn't been written yet."

"Doesn't that mean I'm grandfathered in because the building was already standing there?"

"According to the Illinois statute, the law is invoked after discovery. If you hadn't dug up your house, there wouldn't be a problem."

"If I hadn't had to dig up my house, there wouldn't be a problem because I'd still be living in it, but it burned to the ground. I've spent tens, make that hundreds of thousands of dollars, in permits, plans, fixtures and I have nothing to show for it. I'm living above a store."

"I've filed the papers to begin the excavation. I'm recommending that we hire two archeologists from the University of Illinois to oversee the excavation."

"How long is that going to take?"

"It depends on what they find. We're looking at least a year minimum."

"I can't wait that long."

"You will be responsible for the costs incurred."

"What?" Anne's mouth dropped open. "I didn't put the bones there. Why do I have to pay?"

"Because you own the lot."

"Can I sell the lot?"

"No, not until this is resolved." Jon Berman shook his head.

"I can't live on it. I can't sell it. What am I supposed to do? Doesn't the stay have a protection order for living residents? What about my bones? My bones don't count because I'm still using them?"

Jon tried to hold back his smile. "I'm sorry, Anne, this is the way it is." He paused, and then looked at another folder. "There's one more thing I wanted to talk to you about. I received a letter from your cousin Suzanne's husband's attorney."

"Ex husband," Anne corrected him.

"Actually there were some problems with the court dates for the divorce," Berman said.

"Suzanne led me to believe the divorce was finalized," Anne said.

"The only reason I'm speaking with you about it is because it involves your Aunt Sybil's estate."

"What about it? I thought that had been settled."

"Jack is trying to include the house as part of his divorce settlement. He wants to sell the house and all its contents and split the proceeds with Suzanne."

"He can't do that. It's Suzanne's house. As executor, Aunt Sybil left it up to me to decide who was gifted the house, and I chose Suzanne. Everything was tied up neatly," Anne said.

"He's trying to prove that your Aunt Sybil was not of sound mind when she wrote her will."

"Can he do that?"

"He can try but he won't be successful."

"What about the restraining orders?" Anne asked.

"The restraining order expired."

"He's a dangerous man," Anne said.

"We can't file a restraining order without a cause," Jon Berman said.

"This is getting better and better, isn't it?"

"Oh, and regarding the neighbors' complaints about your building plans. We can try to argue them but my recommendation would be to scale back any future construction."

Anne pictured the to-scale model that Terrence had built her. She had already given up the fourth floor, the turret and the moat. What more could she give up without ruining the aesthetic of her design? And, she had settled for an English craftsman but it was rapidly turning into a small cottage. "Don't tell me anything else. I can't take anymore," she said. "I've written a letter to a friend of mine. He's the chief of the Cherokee nation in North Carolina. He's going to fly out and assess the situation."

"Very good then. We'll end it here for today," Jon said, closing his folder.

Anne left the attorney's office. She had started the morning in a great mood and it had quickly dissipated. How could she revive her spirits? Ingrid was waiting in her Mercedes curbside. Anne hadn't wanted to pay for downtown parking so she had brought her young protégé with her to watch the car.

"Anne, I got a message from one of our fans after I tweeted we were going to be downtown. She lives in the Hancock building."

"That's nice," Anne said.

"What's wrong?"

"I had some bad news. Actually, lots of bad news."

"This will make you feel better. This woman has a lot of Chicago memorabilia. Her father was a cameraman back in the 1960s for GWN."

Anne appeared puzzled. "You mean WGN?"

"Yes, WGN. She said he worked with a lot of famous shows in Chicago, Ray Runder."

"Raynor."

"Garfield Geese."

"Goose."

"Bolo the Clown."

"Bozo. That's very interesting. It's very Chicago. All those shows."

"She has a lot of memorabilia. Old tape recorders and cameras in her storage locker."

"Where's the storage locker?"

"In the Hancock building."

"That's not too far. Can we stop by? Did she tell you what time?"

"I DM'd her and told her we were down here. She gave me her information."

"Mmm, I could use a little fun. Let's go take a look and then we'll eat. I'm starving." Anne glanced sideways at Ingrid's slender athletic physique. Anne had tried her best, although unintentionally, to fatten her up. She had introduced Ingrid to all of Chicago's best fare, deep-dish pizza, hot dogs, beef sandwiches, sliders. None of them put a dent in Ingrid's belt. She had the metabolism of an Olympian. Anne wasn't jealous though. Ingrid was her apprentice. More than apprentice. Anne loved her like a sister, a younger sister—not much younger, but younger. She stared out the window at the Magnificent Mile. She visited these stores regularly. They were old friends. Saks, Neiman, Tiffany, Cartier, Prada. Now her new budget would have to include names like Target, Old Navy and Charming Charlie's. All fine establishments but not magnificent mile-worthy. She drew a deep breath and closed her eyes. She had even more pressing matters in mind. John Blackbear, her on-again, off-again love interest, would be arriving in his private jet tomorrow. The war drums pounded quietly in her ears but this time she realized they weren't imaginary drums. It was her heart pounding not for John Blackbear, but for Nigel Towers. She would have to let John Blackbear down easy.

They pulled up in front of the Hancock building. A young woman was waiting outside for them. Anne jumped out while Ingrid waited in the SUV.

"It is so exciting to meet you in person," Cassie Andrews said. She was nothing like Anne pictured in her skintight jeans, black motorcycle boots and flannel shirt. "The storage lockers are in the basement. Follow me."

"I'll wait in the car in case I have to move it," Ingrid said. Parking on Michigan Avenue was nonexistent.

Anne followed Cassie to the elevator that led to the basement. Their heels clacked on the cement floor, rows of steel cages with numbers lined the walls on either side. Cassie stopped at one and opened the lock. She pulled back the steel gate and switched on a single light bulb hanging from the ceiling.

"You're welcome to any of it," Cassie said waving her hand to the contents.

Anne stepped in. Unlike her storage unit—umm, make that units—this one was neatly organized. Boxes were stacked on top of each other but neatly labeled in black marker. "Bozo's buckets," she read on one. "Cuddly Dudley," she read on another.

She opened the Bozo Bucket box and was instantly brought back to her childhood. Each weekday, Bozo the clown challenged children to throw a ball into staggered buckets to win prizes. Her mother had taken her and her cousin, Suzanne, to the show. *Suzanne,* she thought, *not just her cousin but also her best friend growing up.* Sweet and innocent, full of life, her husband Jack had squeezed that life out of her and now that she had a chance to start a new life, Jack was back in the picture, coming after Aunt Sybil's heirlooms. Not if Anne had anything to say about it. She had stopped him once and this time she'd stop him for good.

"Wow, these are great," she said to Cassie. Box after box revealed items related to her television watching childhood. Cuddly Dudley stuffed animals from *The Ray Rayner Show,* Captain Kangaroo's red jacket and best of all Garfield Goose's crown from *Garfield Goose and Friends.* "How'd you get these?"

"My father was a cameraman for WGN. His camera equipment is on the back shelf there. There are some original microphones, early 1960s. He covered the 1968 Democratic convention riot. It's very interesting. My dad got some footage of the Chicago 8, particularly Abbie Hoffman. WGN didn't air it because it showed the police violence."

"You have the original tape?" Anne asked.

Cassie nodded. "You're welcome to any of this. I'm moving out of state and can't keep dragging everything with me."

"I know how that is," Anne said, picturing the three storage containers she had shipped to the United States from Paris. "We could certainly find homes for all this. Can you bear parting with it?"

Cassie laughed. "It's time. I've been dragging it with me from house to house ever since my dad died. I don't need his stuff to remind me of him. I hold him in my heart."

Anne was impressed. She cherished her stuff that reminded her of all the people who had come in and out of her life. She wasn't sure she could part with any of their belongings, or "stuff," as Cassie called it. "We could take it all off your hands," Anne said.

"That'd be great," Cassie said. "There is one reel that I found. Actually, after I talked to Ingrid, I came and went through the boxes to make sure there was nothing I wanted to keep. I had never seen it before. My father had played many of the reels for me but never this one." Cassie retrieved a round tin case. On it, was a piece of masking tape and handwritten on the tape, "interview with Mayor Daley, October 1971."

Anne glanced at it. "Wow, I'd love to see what's on there."

"That's the funny thing. All the other reel tins are from actual TV cameras. This one is from my dad's personal super 8."

"Why would he use a super 8?"

Cassie shrugged. "I've got my dad's super 8 projector." She retrieved it from the back of the locker. "I've had all the family tapes converted to digital but I've never seen this one until today." Cassie set up the projector and faced it toward the one white wall. She clicked a switch and the light went on. She clicked the second switch and the film wound its way through the projector. A young man with thick black glasses and a clean white shirt popped his head around to the front. "That's my dad," Cassie told Anne.

Cassie's father spoke, "His honor the mayor has agreed to an interview. This is the pre-interview before we bring the full crew in and the television cameras. I'm checking the lighting and deciding where to film his Honor." The camera walked the hallways of City Hall. Two state troopers stood outside Mayor Daley's office door; they opened the door, and the camera went in. The large office was filled with bookshelves, city maps. His honor, the first Mayor Daley, sat behind his big walnut desk. On his desk was a cigar humidor, a football and stacks of books. The mayor looked up at the camera. "Are you getting everything you need, son?" he asked.

"Yes, your Honor."

"That's good."

Anne noticed behind the mayor was an American flag, a state of Illinois flag and a Chicago flag. The camera panned around the office. Then back to the mayor who was busy writing. The camera zoomed in on the mayor. "His tie clip. What's on his tie clip?" she asked.

Cassie went up to the wall to get a closer look. Anne walked up behind her. The mayor was wearing a tie clip with a symbol on it, a symbol that appeared similar to the Ogham lettering on the cedar blanket chest. Anne took out her iPhone and snapped a picture to show CC.

"We can take all of this off your hands," Anne said.

They negotiated a price, found a flatbed dolly, loaded it up and brought it out to Anne's SUV. Once they had fit everything they could into the vehicle, they made arrangements for Adam and Nick to come pick up everything else.

"Killer find," Anne told Ingrid as she settled back in the passenger seat. "Now, lunch." They drove along Michigan Avenue. Anne's thoughts turned to food. Her low-carb diet was put on hold with thoughts of Chicago's famous stuffed pizza at Gino's East. She decided to bypass that temptation. Then she thought about Lawry's where you could hand pick your steak cooked to order. Steak was low carb. She felt good about that decision, but her pocketbook had just taken a considerable hit. "How do you feel about McDonald's?" Anne asked Ingrid.

"Really?" Ingrid asked.

"It's not any McDonald's," Anne said. "It's the Rock and Roll McDonald's, a Chicago landmark. Have you ever had McDonald's?"

"Yes, I'm from Germany, not from the rainforest."

"Let's grab a bite and then we'll bring this stuff to the store. I want to sort through it," Anne said, not adding that she wanted to sort through it before CC could stop her.

After ordering, they sat at a booth surrounded by tourists and a life-size Elvis. "How are things with Adam?" Anne asked. "We don't see much of you anymore outside of the store."

"I've been busy with school and homework and studying."

"Yes, yes, yes, but what about Adam?" Anne poured ketchup on her fries.

"We've put things on hold."

"Why? He's so nice and handsome."

"I. . . I do like him. I like him a lot but he's getting really serious. He was talking about marriage."

"Oh? I didn't realize."

"I'm not ready for that kind of commitment."

"Gosh, no. Me either."

"So I'm going to be spending more time at work with you. And I've got a month before the fall semester starts. I was hoping we could hit some estate sales and you could continue training me."

Anne looked up from her Big Mac. "I'd be delighted." Anne's phone pinged. She glanced down at the text message. "Where are you?" it read in all caps. Anne turned a guilty look toward Ingrid. "We forgot CC. She's at the Water Tower. We were supposed to pick her up after we met with the attorney."

"Oops," Ingrid said. They hurriedly finished their lunch and got in the car. They drove back to Michigan Avenue where CC was standing at the curb, tapping her foot in front of the yellowing Joliet limestone Water Tower, one of the only buildings to survive the Great Fire.

"Where'd you go? And what are all these boxes?" CC asked, climbing on top of three boxes and scrunching down to keep her head from hitting the roof of the car.

"After I went to the attorney, Ingrid found a fan who lives down here. She was selling all her collectibles. I bought everything," Anne said, sipping at her chocolate shake. "How was your afternoon?" she asked, trying to change the subject.

"Very interesting," CC said. "You know, Anne and Ingrid, the Chicago Water Tower was constructed in 1869 to house a large water pump intended to draw water from Lake Michigan. William W. Boyington designed it. There's a 138-foot standpipe to hold water inside. Besides its use for firefighting, the pressure in the pipe could be regulated to control water surges in the area. The tower is the only public building in the burn zone to survive."

"How was your research?" Anne wanted to avoid the rest of the history lesson.

CC brought up her photo gallery on her iPhone. She leaned forward from her perch on the cardboard boxes to show Anne.

"What is that, CC?"

"This is carved into the cornerstone. It's the Ogham symbol for elm." She enlarged the picture so Anne could see it better.

"Oh, wait," Anne said, pulling out her phone and handing it to CC. "I took this photo from an old film reel Cassie had of her father interviewing Mayor Daley. Her father was a WGN cameraman. Look at the mayor's tie clip."

CC looked closely at the Ogham symbol for elm, the same one she had seen in the water tower and on the fire truck at the Sanfillipo estate. "That symbol. That's the same Ogham symbol for elm. It was on the fire truck at the estate. Wayne explained that it was used to memorialize the seven firefighters who died in the Chicago fire."

"Why the elm tree?" Anne asked.

"Because they died evacuating Marshall Field's mansion on Elm Street."

"Why would Mayor Daley be wearing the elm symbol?"

"The Chicago fire department was comprised mainly of Irish immigrants," CC said. "Mayor Daley was Irish and a leader in the community. It wouldn't be so far-fetched to see him wearing an Irish symbol."

"Yes, but why elm? Why the elm tree?" Anne asked. "What's his connection, if any, with Marshall Field and the Chicago fire?"

CC had no answer but instead Googled 1971 Mayor Daley. The first thing that came up was a photo of Mayor Daley at his inaugural address in April 1971. CC read the beginning of his speech out loud, "My employer is all the people of Chicago, Democrats, Republicans, and independents of every economic group, of every neighborhood... We must constantly improve our police and fire departments." CC skimmed through the rest of the speech and then brought up images of the ceremony. Posed behind Mayor Daley were the Police Chief, Fire Chief and a man she didn't recognize. She scrolled down to the caption where he was identified as Marshall Field V. She enlarged the image. They all wore the same tie clip with the Ogham symbol for elm. CC held the phone in front to show Anne.

"All the same tie clip," Anne said.

"Marshall Field must have given the mayor the tie clip as an inaugural gift. 1971 was also the hundredth anniversary of the Chicago Fire," CC said. "A thank you to the city of Chicago for saving the family business."

Anne slurped her empty milkshake cup, pondering the significance.

"I'm positive now that the scrollwork on the lantern was Ogham symbols." CC put her hand on top of her head to stop it from hitting the roof.

"How does this all tie in with Patricia Rounder?"

"Nigel said that Patricia was wanted by the Irish police yet she was a British citizen. She was carrying a lantern inscribed with an ancient Irish language, a lantern that she had with her when she was killed. The only possession she carried across the sea was that lantern. If we find the lantern, we can figure out what the symbols mean and possibly the identity of her killer. First, we have to find out all the details of Patricia's crime in Ireland and why she was there."

"So, we're going to Ireland?" Anne asked.

"No, don't be silly. We're going to Google."

Chapter Twenty-Six

Anne stood next to the tall, weathered, handsome John Blackbear. Seeing him again made her heart beat a little faster. One frantic text message and Blackbear had rushed to her aid. "See, John, this is where the house used to stand." Anne pointed to the enormous hole in the ground which was now surrounded by excavating equipment. The two archeologists were down in the hole, using fine brushes to dust off the remains.

"I see, Anne." Chief John Blackbear climbed down into the former foundation. Anne watched as he spoke to the archeologists. From her vantage point above, she could not hear what he was saying or their reply.

He bent down, touched something in the soft dirt, dusted his hands off and then climbed back up to her. "Anne, they said it is definitely a Winnebago tribal burial ground," he said.

"Can you help me? I need to get my house built," she said.

"Anne, the Winnebago are part of the Sioux nation. I'm Cherokee. I have no influence with the Sioux. Even if I did, it's a state matter and it's sacred ground; I wouldn't disturb it."

Anne sighed, trying to conceal her frustration. "I don't understand. Why did you fly all the way out here when you knew you wouldn't be able to help me?"

"I wanted to see you face to face. I have something to talk to you about."

*Oh, no*, Anne thought, *he's going to ask me to marry him.* What about Nigel? I have to let Blackbear down easy. "You can tell me over dinner," Anne said. She took Blackbear by the arm and walked back to her Mercedes.

Anne headed down to Lawry's Steakhouse. She had been dreaming of their steaks since Ingrid and she had passed by the restaurant. She was on a budget but John Blackbear wasn't. She would let him down easy over a blue cheese crusted filet mignon. Oh, and lobster tail.

The valet took their car as John Blackbear led her into the restaurant, his hand on her back. Housed in the former McCormick mansion, Lawry's coffered ceiling and crystal chandelier loomed over Anne's head. She glanced up, marveling at its beauty. All features she had been forced to give up in her steadily shrinking Hillstrom Manor.

They sat at a table and John Blackbear ordered a bottle of red wine. "Your jet is beautiful," Anne said. When she'd picked up John, he had given her a tour of his new G5.

"It actually belongs to the casino."

"Yes, but you own the casino."

"My people do but they allow me to have the jet at my disposal."

"It's really lovely."

John Blackbear interrupted her and took her hand in his. "Anne, I wanted to talk to you."

Anne pulled her hand out of his, sipped her water and held her finger up. "John, before you say anything. I wanted to talk to you."

"I'm getting back together with my ex-wife," John Blackbear blurted out.

Anne choked on her water, coughing.

"Are you all right?" John Blackbear asked.

Anne coughed again, holding her hand up. "I'm fine. Your ex-wife? How? When? Why?"

"She's been visiting family back in Cherokee, and we've been seeing a lot of each other. As we grow older, we understand that many of our differences don't really matter. We've always had a good working relationship but our personal relationship suffered because of it. That caused us to grow apart but now we've been able to work through those differences."

"But, what about us?" Anne asked realizing that somehow she had lost her appetite.

John Blackbear took Anne's hands into his large hand. He smiled, his brown eyes sparkling. "I've cherished our relationship. You've breathed life back into me. In fact, being with you made me realize how much I missed being in a relationship."

"Oh?" Suddenly all she could think of was how to get him back. Forget Nigel. John Blackbear was all she wanted. The waiter brought over their steaks. Anne was so upset she was only able to eat half her steak but she managed to eat the entire lobster tail because it was the right thing to do. For the rest of the dinner, they remained silent.

"Dessert, Anne?"

"What?" she asked.

"Would you like some dessert?"

She glanced over to see the silver cart full of delicious temptations. She knew from experience how delicious they were. She looked at the dessert and then over to John Blackbear and then at the dessert cart again. She was hungry for both. She had worked hard on her low carb, paleo, whole 30 diet to get back into her fighting weight. Now there was nothing to fight for. John Blackbear was lost. His ex-wife the winner. Anne chose the fresh made cheesecake and the hot fudge sundae. If she was down for the count, she was going to enjoy it.

John Blackbear smiled. He enjoyed seeing a woman with a healthy appetite. It was one of the things that had attracted him to Anne, her lust for life.

When they were finished eating, she asked, "Are you flying back this evening?"

"I don't have any plans. My schedule is pretty open."

She glanced up from her cheesecake. His broad shoulders, his chiseled chin, those eyes she had gotten lost in. She needed more time. "John, have you ever been to Ireland?"

Chapter Twenty-Seven

Anne reveled in the luxury of John's private jet. They were midway over the Atlantic. CC was typing on her iPad mini, filing a story on steel prices. Ingrid was ignoring texts from Adam. John Blackbear sat across from Anne, sipping a single malt scotch. "So, Anne, you haven't said much about why we're flying to Ireland, so why are we?"

Anne stood up and sat next to John on the couch. She had managed to fit into her vintage Mary Quant miniskirt and a crop top. One of the perks of her Swedish Viking blood, she forever looked young and could pull off the look. Though she couldn't pull off the four-inch heels for that long. Those came off as soon as they boarded. She inched closer to John until her thigh rested against his. She could tell he was eying her. She was pulling out all the stops. "John, I guess I never told you about Patricia Rounder. She was a fan of our blog. She came to our store several weeks ago carrying a lantern and died in my arms."

"Anne, I'm so sorry to hear that. How did she die?"

"She died of a stab wound. We don't know much more than that except that the Irish police wanted her for murder. She was a British citizen but apparently committed a murder in Ireland." Anne didn't know any more details. *The less drama, the better,* she thought. "Anyway, we're going to Wexford. CC was able to find out that the warrant for her arrest was issued from Wexford County. It's in the southeast, a big farming and dairy community."

"What do you hope to find?"

"I watched this woman die." Anne said, remembering that storm filled night. "I want to know more about her. Who she was and why the lantern was so important to her."

John Blackbear pulled a cigar out of his shirt pocket. He gave Anne a nod, asking for approval. She gave it. He lit up the cigar. "Well, then, we'll have to find out."

Anne gave him a kiss on the cheek. "Thank you."

CC watched the whole exchange between John Blackbear and Anne. She was wearing her noise cancelling earphones but she shut them off so she could listen to their conversation. CC stared out the window as the emerald green cliffs appeared.

A few hours later, they entered the two-story brick Wexford Garda station.

CC took over. "May we speak to the detective handling the Patricia Rounder case?" she asked, not sure if police procedurals were the same in Ireland as in the United States.

A short while later, a red-haired fireplug of a man came up to the day desk. "I'm Inspector Shannon. And you are?"

CC showed him her press pass. He checked it over. "What's an American journalist doing in Ireland asking questions about Patricia Rounder?"

"Patricia Rounder died in our antique store," CC replied.

"Come back to my office," he said.

They all filed up to the second floor. Anne was definitely regretting her heels. Why hadn't she packed another pair of shoes? Or, why couldn't they have taken the elevator? They went into the detective's office. "This is my friend and business partner, Anne Hillstrom, my cousin, Ingrid Muller, and this is John Blackbear," CC introduced everyone.

Inspector Shannon gave Blackbear an eye. He had a way of standing out in a crowd. Inspector Shannon opened a file drawer and pulled out a large thick folder. "Yes, I spoke with Detective Phillips of the Glen Ellyn Police Force." He looked up at CC. "There's not much I can tell you about Patricia Rounder. She wasn't from the area. She was a drifter."

"She was a British citizen yet the warrant was a Garda warrant," CC said.

The inspector stood up, shut the door and sat back down. "She was wanted for questioning in a murder case," he said.

"I wasn't able to find out any information on the warrant other than it was from Wexford," CC said.

"There was a break-in at a local dairy farm. Nothing was taken except the pick-up truck. The farmer must have tried to stop the thief."

"How was he killed?" CC asked.

"He had a heart attack."

"That's terrible," Anne said.

"Why did you suspect Patricia Rounder?" CC asked.

"She had served time at the Askham Grange in North Yorkshire for breaking and entering and auto theft. She broke her parole by leaving the country, a local garda spotted her in a pub in Wexford but she escaped."

"Why would she come to Wexford?"

"We don't know."

"Did the farmer have any family?"

"Yes, his wife, Sharon, runs the farm."

CC thought for a moment. She couldn't think of anything else to ask him. "Thank you. You've been very helpful."

"Let me show you out," the inspector said, opening the door. On their way back downstairs, he asked, "Will you be in Wexford long?"

"We're here for a short trip. By the way, what was the farmer's name?" CC asked.

"Patrick O'Leary," he said.

Chapter Twenty-Eight

John Blackbear drove the Range Rover down the dirt road through the rolling green hills dotted with jersey cows. "Oh, John, while we are here, we have to go to the Loftus House," Anne said, reading from one of the brochures she had picked up in town. "It's the most haunted house in Ireland. Oh, and CC, you're going to love this. The Irish master of woodturning is in Wexford. We should check out his gallery."

"Anne, how long do you think we're going to be here?" CC asked.

Ingrid never raised her head from her iPhone.

"Adam's not giving up, is he?" Anne asked.

Ingrid shook her head.

"You're too young to be in a serious relationship. You have to think about school and your career," Anne said.

Ingrid glanced up from her phone. "I don't want to be 40 years old and single with no kids," she hesitated. "Oh, CC, I'm so sorry, I didn't mean anything."

CC interrupted, "No, that's okay. This is the path I chose. I'm happy with it." At one time, CC had dreamed of having a houseful of children but it had never quite worked out between her and her ex. She had focused on her career. Now she was happy to play second mother to Ingrid.

"We're here," Anne said, breaking through the tension building in the backseat between the two cousins. They pulled up to a stone cottage, surrounded by acres and acres of green gulleys and running streams. The cottage broke through the morning mist like the enchanted village of Brigadoon.

CC half expected to see a hobbit answer the door when she knocked. The woman who answered was a bit taller than a hobbit but not by much. She was plump and rosy cheeked and like many of the Wexfordians, red haired and freckled. "Hello, may I help you?"

"I'm CC Muller, a journalist from Chicago. Inspector Shannon gave me your name."

"Oh, yes, the inspector, please come in. I was having tea." The tiny woman looked up at John Blackbear who had to duck his head to enter the doorway. "Please sit down." She led them to a small wooden kitchen table. She bustled around the kitchen, setting cups and tea on the counter as well as Irish soda bread. "Why are you here?"

"My friend and partner, Anne Hillstrom." CC pointed to Anne, who was slathering butter on a large piece of bread. "We own an antique store outside Chicago. Patricia Rounder showed up at our store and collapsed dead."

"That serves that horrible woman right. She took my Patrick." The woman closed her eyes, obviously holding back tears.

"Inspector Shannon said that Patricia was wanted for questioning but did not go into details of the crime," CC said.

"I told the inspector everything that happened that night. I never saw the thief. The gardai told me they thought it was this woman. She was a fugitive and was seen in the area."

"Can you tell me about that night?"

"It was about four weeks to the day. My husband and I were sound asleep when a noise from the barn woke us. Patrick grabbed his walking stick and ran out to see what was going on. He told me to stay in the house. I ran to the porch when I heard the truck spin out just in time to see the thief taking off in the truck and my Patrick laying on the ground," Sharon said.

"So you never got a good look at the driver?" CC asked.

"From what I could see of her, the description fit Patricia Rounder. My Patrick had a troubled heart. It was too much for him. He died the next morning."

"I'm sorry for your loss. So Patrick died of a heart attack? He wasn't run over by the truck?"

The woman stopped and grabbed the teakettle. "She might not have killed him but she caused his death. All to steal a rusty old pick-up truck. We're not wealthy people. We don't have a lot. Why would someone want to steal from us?"

"Was there anything taken from the barn?" CC asked.

"Just an old lantern that had been on the farm for years. It didn't even work," Sharon said.

"Why would someone take a lantern?" CC asked.

Sharon poured tea and shook her head. "I don't know."

"And that's all that she took?"

"Patrick tried to stop her. She didn't have time to take much more, not that there's much to take. And now he lies dead in the family plot over the hill there. I walk there every morning with fresh flowers for his grave." She dabbed at her eyes with her handkerchief. CC could see the tears welling up in Sharon's eyes. She had never experienced the kind of love that this woman must be feeling. It made her sad for the woman and sad for herself. "I was going to bring flowers down. Do you want to come with me?"

"We can pay our respects," CC said.

They walked down the narrow cobblestone path that ended at the family cemetery, which was surrounded by a wrought iron fence. A little archway adorned with angels marked the entrance. CC admired the craftsmanship. The woman led them to her husband's grave and placed a small bouquet of forget-me-nots by his headstone. They all bowed their heads. CC looked around the plot at the other headstones, some dating back to the 1700s, and pre-Irish rebellion. Sharon knelt down, did the sign of the cross and murmured a prayer. She looked over at CC who was examining one of the headstones. "Yes, that's Patrick's four times grandfather. He died in the rebellion. That one there died during the potato famine. Many of the O'Learys went to America during the famine."

CC noticed a headstone inscribed, "Patrick O'Leary, 1940."

"Was he a soldier?"

"Oh, my Patrick's great-uncle, one of the American O'Leary's. He was a brilliant man, a mechanical engineer in the army. He was angry that America didn't join the fight quick enough so he came here and signed up in 1939. He was British intelligence," Sharon said, pulling weeds from around her husband's grave.

"Really? That's interesting." CC said.

"From what I know of Patrick he was quite the puzzler and a champion chess player," Sharon said. "He worked on the enigma project as a code breaker. He helped build the machine that broke the Nazi code."

CC wiped the moss away from the headstone. That's when she saw the inscription written in Ogham. "Sharon, what does this sentence mean?"

"Roughly translated, it's an old Celtic blessing. Something like the key to enlightenment lies down a narrow path." Sharon went back to tending her husband's grave.

CC stared at the Ogham symbol for elm tree. She gazed up at the willow tree that was swaying gracefully in the heart of the cemetery. "How are the angels going to find Patrick?"

Sharon smiled and said, "Oh, you know the old tradition? How we mark the headstones with the symbol of the burial tree? Patrick carved that headstone himself."

"That's rather macabre," CC said.

"No, this was not unusual for the young lads who were going to war to prepare for the worst. I've always thought it a bit peculiar that he carved it with an elm not a willow tree, but that's who Patrick was. As I said, Patrick was a riddler, a puzzler. I'm sure it was his way of making it more difficult for the angels to find him. He wanted them to work for it, to solve the puzzle," she said.

CC took a picture of the headstone. As she flipped through her photo gallery, she came to a picture of the lantern she had taken. Some of the lattice engraving on its bottom matched the headstone, but the one symbol that stood out was the one for elm tree.

When it was time to go, Sharon led them out of the small graveyard. As CC passed under the archway, she looked up at one of the angels, which was holding a key. Something about the key struck her. It was more than a decorative key. It had several intricate tumbler teeth. She brought up the picture of the lantern and the close-up of its lock that held the lattice sleeve. The keyhole had the same intricate pattern. She reached up and snapped the key, pulling it out of the angel's hand. It came out easily as though it was made to do so. Engraved on the back of the key was the Ogham symbol for an elm tree. She put it in her purse. She turned around, faced the graveyard and made the sign of the cross, "Forgive me," she said.

Chapter Twenty-Eight

"Where's Anne? We have a long drive ahead of us," CC asked, getting back in the Rover.

John Blackbear pointed ahead. They had stopped for petrol at a gas station in a quaint Irish village. CC turned her eye to where he pointed. "Oh, no," she said, seeing the sign that read "Custom Precious Jewelry." The one next to it read "Heirloom Celtic Robes." The next shop read, "Wood Turning." CC surveyed the street. Both sides were lined with picturesque art galleries, rug shops and custom jewelers. "Which one did she go to?" CC asked. She had to stop her friend before it was too late.

John Blackbear simply pointed again. CC followed the direction of his finger. She jumped back out of the car, ran to the shop and flew in. "Oh, Anne, it's beautiful," she heard Ingrid say.

"Anne, what are you doing?" CC asked.

Both Anne and Ingrid turned to stare at CC. Around Anne's neck was an enormous gold necklace with a single large amethyst. "Isn't it grand, CC?" Anne asked.

"Yes, it is." CC reached over, grabbing Anne's arm, pulling her to the corner of the shop. "What are you doing? You can't afford any of this."

"Don't worry, CC, it's not that expensive. It's like 20 of these things." Anne pulled a wad of Euros out of her pocket.

"They're euros. They're real money. Besides, you have a house to build," CC reminded her.

"Oh, I bought a beautiful tapestry and matching rug for the house already. They're shipping it to your house so we don't have to carry it back. I wanted to buy something for me and for Ingrid to remember our trip to Ireland."

Ingrid flashed her hand to show a small but elaborately set blue topaz ring. "I think we'll take both pieces," Anne said, taking the necklace off and setting it on the counter.

After she had paid, Anne stepped out onto the street with Ingrid and CC. Her arms held several small shopping bags. "Where should we go next? Mmm, perhaps some coffee or pastry?" she said.

"We have to go. We have a long drive ahead of us," CC said, leading them to the Range Rover where John Blackbear was waiting patiently. "John," CC said, tapping on the window. "You've been very generous. Can I ask you to extend your generosity for one more day?"

Chapter Twenty-Nine

"You know, Anne, Bletchley Park was the site of the government's code and cipher school during World War II. Top minds from around the world worked on breaking the German enigma code," CC said. "This is where Turing created the bombe, an early computer."

They entered through the white iron gate that led onto a circular driveway. "You know, Anne, in 1883 Herbert Samuel Leon, a wealthy London financier, built this mansion on 300 acres."

Anne stared at the multi-gabled expansive building. She pictured similar gables on her current English craftsman design.

"In 1938, the government acquired the mansion and the land to use as headquarters for their code breaking operations." CC continued, consulting her guidebook, "The enigma was the backbone of Germany military intelligence communications. It was invented in 1918. It was initially designed to secure banking communications."

"Several of these huts, outbuildings, were used to house the code breakers and mathematicians. There was a women's quarters for the women who intercepted the German messages. What we're looking for should be in here, Anne," CC said, consulting her guidebook. A plaque outside the building said Hut 11. "Bombe Rebuild Project Display Area." "All of the original bombes, as they were called, were basically simple computers that were destroyed in World War II," CC said. "The Museum has reconstructed an exact replica of Turing's original bombe."

"CC, I would never turn down a chance to visit London," Anne said before momentarily picturing antique shopping in Piccadilly and visiting her old friends, the crown jewels in the Tower. "Bletchley Park is fascinating but why are we here?"

CC glanced around the commons area. Ingrid was sitting on a bench next to John Blackbear, deep in conversation. "Anne, when we were in the graveyard, I found a headstone with Patrick O'Leary's name inscribed on it. It had an Ogham inscription that Sharon translated as 'the key to enlightenment lies down a narrow path.'" CC took the key out she had borrowed from the graveyard.

"What's that?" Anne asked.

"This key was in the angel's hand in the archway of the cemetery which transversed the narrow path we walked," CC said.

"But, CC—"

CC brought up the picture of the lantern on her iPhone. "The tumbler teeth all line up with the keyhole on the lantern that locks the scrolled sleeve in place."

"That's quite a stretch," Anne said.

"The lantern and the gravestone had the same Ogham inscriptions. Patrick O'Leary was a mechanical engineer who worked on breaking the enigma code here in Bletchley Park."

"Ohmigosh," Anne said.

"We need to find out who Patrick O'Leary was and why this key was so important to him."

Anne looked behind CC. towards the bench where Ingrid and John Blackbear were deep in conversation. "What are John Blackbear and Ingrid talking about?"

"I don't know but they were huddled up on the plane ride whispering about something." CC waved over to the bench.

Ingrid held her hand up and shook her head. Anne and CC went into the hut. Much of the building was reconstructed exactly as it stood in 1940. Plaques and interactive displays hung on the wall. Photos included the code breakers and a big portrait of Alan Turing. In the center of the hut, roped off, was the replica of the original Turing bombe, code-breaking computer.

"I didn't think it would be this big," Anne said.

"It weighs nearly a ton. It's all electrical, mechanical moving parts." CC wandered around, studying its tumblers and shafts. "It's quite remarkable for the 1940s." A tour of schoolchildren walked by.

"What are you looking for?" Anne asked.

After looking around her, CC snuck under the velvet rope. Anne whispered, "What are you doing?"

"Keep an eye out," CC said as she went to the back of the machine. She examined the access panels and the hundreds of feet of cables. She ran her hand along the main power cord. She hoped that this truly was an exact replica of the machine that Patrick O'Leary worked on. Some of the steel panels were original from the first machine. CC could tell the age between those and the reconstructed steel from the oxidation and texture even as she touched them. One panel held the answer to the question she was asking. Written in Ogham, the same inscription that lay over Patrick O'Leary's head, "the key to enlightenment lies down a narrow path" and the symbol for an elm tree. She snapped a photo and ran back under the velvet rope. Anne was nowhere to be found. "Anne, where are you?" CC called out.

She traveled down a narrow hallway to find a room with video monitors. "CC, come here, this is really interesting," Anne said.

She was standing in front of a video monitor watching old film reels. "These are actual films of some of the code breakers and the women who were intercepting the German U-boat messages," Anne said.

A title, "Patrick O'Leary, mechanical engineer," flashed on the screen. CC and Anne watched the ghost of Patrick O'Leary as he explained the calibration of the bombe's code tumblers. Alan Turing stood near him quietly. Patrick spoke, "The key to deciphering this code lies down this narrow path of electrical gears which rotate the shafts. Timing them exactly will enable us to decipher the encryptions much faster."

The next part of the film showed Alan Turing and Patrick O'Leary playing chess in the courtyard and Patrick winning.

CC stood transfixed, staring at the monitor as 1960 flashed on the screen. A pretty middle-aged woman was being interviewed by an off-screen voice. "Tell us your name," the interviewer asked.

The woman smiled. "Joyce Rounder."

"What was your occupation during the war?"

"I helped transcribe intercepted messages."

"What was your background? What brought you to Bletchley Park?"

"I was a secretary in London. They needed help during the war. I was an expert at the *Daily London* crossword puzzle. I won many contests. I think that's what put me on their radar. I'm a bit of a fanatic when it comes to puzzles and riddles. A lot of the girls and the engineers I worked with were recruited because we liked to solve puzzles."

The voice asked. "Did you live in the women's quarters?"

"Yes, I was single at the time I worked here."

"What was it like working and living here during the war?"

"There was a great camaraderie, a sense of purpose, you might say. All the girls became quite close, like sisters."

"What about the young men?"

A wily smile crept across her face. "What about the men?" She then spoke directly into the camera. "The boys had the same camaraderie. I remember a Christmas party in 1939. It was actually more of a dance. I danced with a young engineer, a handsome boy, not more than 21 years old. He died in a bombing in September 1940."

"What was his name?"

Suddenly her smile turned to a frown, a shadow crossed her face. "His name was Patrick O'Leary," she said. The video ended.

"Patricia Rounder was Patrick O'Leary's daughter," Anne said, gasping.

"That's why she went to the O'Leary farm. She knew about the lantern but not the key," CC said.

"And somebody killed her because of it," Anne said, shivering.

"And now they know we know."

Anne and CC hurried out of the building and to the park bench where Ingrid was sitting with John Blackbear. CC sat down next to Ingrid.

Anne reached out her hand to John Blackbear. "John, let's take a walk," she said. They walked down the path near a lagoon under a canopy of old massive oak trees. Sprinkled in between were violets and meadow sage which swayed in the afternoon breeze. Anne stopped and turned, gazing up at John. In the near past, this would have been enough for John to take her in his arms but he stood still looking down at her.

"Anne, I feel you don't quite understand my relationship with my ex-wife. It wasn't my decision to separate and I never stopped loving her," he said.

Anne listened to the words but John's eyes were telling a different story. All of her life Anne Hillstrom had longed for what she couldn't have. The harder it was to obtain, the more she required it. Standing in front of her was the unattainable. She buried her cheek into his chest. He put his arms around her. As she pulled back from his hold, she saw a British bobby walking down the pathway, twirling his baton. It made her smile. It was so perfectly British just like Nigel. *Nigel*, she thought, *what was she doing? Nigel should be here with her. They should be walking hand in hand, laughing.*

John Blackbear leaned over to kiss Anne. She stopped him. "You're right, John, I've not been fair to you. I'm still very attracted to you. I love being with you, but I'm not the love of your life. You deserve to have that kind of love and so do I."

CC and Ingrid watched in silence from the bench, trying to imagine what the two were speaking about. CC turned to Ingrid. "What were you and John Blackbear discussing? It seemed very intense."

"He told me that when he first came to the shop, he was going to ask Anne to marry him."

"No," CC gasped. "What stopped him?"

"His ex-wife. She had called him as he was driving up to Chicago. She told him that she'd been miserable without him and she wanted to give the relationship another chance."

"Oh, that's probably what they're talking about right now," CC said.

"He also asked me if I wanted to work for him."

"What do you mean work for him?"

"He's been reading the Spoon Sister blogs and especially my posts. His wife, his ex-wife, is moving back and she wants to redecorate the house."

"He wants you to help?" CC asked.

"Yes, he really likes my style. A lot of the antiques I posted captured his wife's interest."

"Oh," CC said.

"I told him that I couldn't possibly do it without you and Anne."

"Oh. We don't need to talk about it now," CC said. "I think it's going to be a long flight home."

Chapter Thirty

Waiting on the tarmac at Midway Airport, CC watched as Anne hugged John Blackbear goodbye. Anne's embrace lasted a few uncomfortable minutes too long. As with most things in Anne's life, she had a hard time letting go. Anne stood, watching the jet take off, holding one hand in the air for a final goodbye. CC put her arm around her friend. Ingrid hugged both of them.

CC felt the key in her pocket. "Anne, something's been bothering me," she said.

"Yeah, me, too," Anne said as she caught a last glimpse of the jet's tail as it disappeared in a vapor trail.

"No, Anne." CC pulled the key out. "Patrick's headstone is underneath a willow tree, not an elm tree."

Anne turned around and stared CC in the eyes. "And, why does that bother you, CC?"

She held the key up. "This symbol keeps popping up everywhere, Anne. I think we need to trace this family tree," CC said, "no pun intended, back to its roots."

"What are you talking about? Do you have jet lag? You're not making any sense."

"I'm talking about taking a drive to Mount Olivet."

A short while later, they drove through the gate of the cemetery on 111th Street. They pulled in the entrance way between the stone pillars. "CC, it's going to be dark soon. I'm sure they're closing." They drove down the rows of headstones. CC stuck her head out, trying to read the markers. "Anne, slow down. Wait, stop."

Anne slammed on the brakes, forcing CC to hit the dashboard. "Anne, really?" CC jumped out, opening the door, running over to an old grave. She read the name out loud, "James J. Bell. Anne, James Bell, is a Medal of Honor recipient. He was a private in the Seventh Cavalry at Big Horn in 1876." She walked down the rows. "Oh, Anne, John J. Pharrel, March 24, 1918. Anne, he's a major league baseball player known as Chick. This is before the Cubs were the Cubs. Here's Thomas H. Jordan, 1840-1930, Civil War Congressional Medal of Honor recipient, a quartermaster in the Union Navy. I wish I had my rice paper and crayon so I could make some etchings."

Ingrid stood patiently while CC walked up and down the headstones. Anne stood not so patiently, watching the sun set and her eBay watch list. "CC, I don't want to be here after dark. Can we get going?"

"Anne, you know Al Capone was buried here, right? Somebody tried to dig him up so they moved him."

Anne put her phone down. The trees cast a long shadow dancing over the graves. It was ghostly quiet. The last sparkle of sunlight was choked out by the tall ash and linden trees surrounding the final headstone CC was standing over. "This is it, Anne," she said.

Anne crept up and peeked over CC's shoulder. She read the name, "Catherine O'Leary, 1827 to July 3, 1895. Anne, look! The Ogham symbol for *elm*." CC touched the linden tree next to the grave. "Not an elm to be had, Anne, not a single elm," she said.

Chapter Thirty-One

"Put that down," CC said as Anne swerved toward the shoulder of the highway.

"It's Berman, my attorney," Anne said, switching her eyes between the road and her iPhone.

"Hand me the phone. What's going on with the house?" CC asked.

"They found another skeleton. This one was a chief, full headdress, the whole bit. And even worse, he had beaded jewelry with him that has to go to the museum even though it was on my property," Anne complained.

"Well, Anne, technically it's not really your property. The Winnebago settled here a thousand years before you."

"They weren't trying to build an English craftsman on it, were they?"

CC laughed. "Probably not. Don't you think it's time you gave up on that lot and you donate it for the tax write off?"

"Where am I going to live? What about Grandma Jan? How could I move away from her and Snowball? What about all the fixtures, hardware, tile, furniture that I already bought?"

"Where is all this stuff?"

"Well, I might have bought a storage facility, just a small one, that technically we can use for the store also. See, it's an investment. It's in unincorporated Glen Ellyn."

CC thought for a moment. "That's actually not a bad idea."

'See, I'm trying to be practical, CC."

"Speaking of practical, what was that conversation you had with John Blackbear?"

"John is getting back with his ex-wife."

"I know that. Ingrid told me."

"How did Ingrid know?"

"John's ex-wife wants Ingrid to decorate their house in North Carolina."

"What? What are you talking about?" Anne was shocked. After all they had been through, how could John Blackbear ignore her experience and ask Ingrid to decorate his house?

"He's become a big fan of the blog and enjoys reading Ingrid's posts," CC said.

"Ingrid's posts? What about my posts?"

"Maybe he didn't feel comfortable asking his ex-fling to decorate his ex-wife, soon-to-be-current wife's house?"

"Oh, yeah, I guess that makes sense." Anne stopped for a moment and changed the subject. "Why are we going up to the Bee's Knees?"

CC pulled the key out of her purse. "Patrick O'Leary made this key. I'm also convinced he created the sleeve around the lantern."

"Yeah, but the lantern's gone. Catherine said it was stolen from her porch."

"I don't believe it was stolen," CC said. "I believe whoever chased us through the cornfields has the lantern and is after the key."

"So, you think that Catherine's involved?"

"If she's not, then she knows who might be." As they turned down the gravel access road leading to the Bee's Knees, they saw a backhoe digging up the cornfield. "That's strange. It's too early to clear the fields. The corn's not ready yet."

"Catherine said they were digging irrigation ditches. I saw them all over the farm when we were here the first time," Anne said, narrowly scraping the side of the SUV against the fence.

On the farm entrance hung a "closed" sign, and the gate was locked with a padlock. "I thought they were open on Saturdays," Anne said, stopping the car.

"I did, too." CC jumped out of the Mercedes.

"What are you doing?"

She reached into her purse and took out her ring of skeleton keys. She tried several keys until one finally popped the old padlock. "Let's go." They walked up the long driveway, stopping at the little open market store. All the bins were empty, several were turned over. "This should be full of strawberries and tomatoes this time of year."

They went up the steps to the front door. CC peeked in the window and tried the knob. It was locked. "Something doesn't feel right, Anne."

She tried the knob again and the door swung open. "CC, you can't go in there," Anne said.

"I'm going to stick my head in to see what's going on."

Peeking into the dark hallway, her eyes adjusted to the dim light. She couldn't make out anything. Stepping in, she heard a crunch under her foot. It was shards of a honey jar. "I don't like this," Anne said.

CC continued on, heading into the kitchen to see flies buzzing around. Dirty dishes piled in the sink. "This isn't right." Anne stood behind her.

They tiptoed up the stairs adjoining the kitchen to the second floor, glancing in each bedroom, calling out Catherine's name. CC got to the last bedroom, the master bedroom. Catherine's canopy bed was unmade. The wind was blowing from the southeast lifting her window sheers up and off the windowsill. A rocking chair swayed slowly from the afternoon breeze, giving the room an eerie presence. The chair sat empty by the window, a small table next to it held an open book. The afternoon light lit up the corner of the room.

All the drawers in her dresser were open, clothes spilling over. "Catherine kept a neat house. Wherever she's gone to, she wouldn't have left her room like this," CC said.

Anne went into the closet. It was full of sundresses, boots and hatboxes. As she went up on her tiptoes to grab an old Charles A. Stevens' hatbox from the top shelf, the old oak plank floor creaked under her feet. She hopped on the floor. It creaked some more. Her first thought was her diet. Then she realized that was the only section of floor creaking. She reached up for the single light bulb that was hanging overhead and pulled the chain. There was no light to be had. Turning on the flashlight app on her iPhone, she picked up the small round braided rug on the floor. She ran her hand along the planks. One of them was loose. She popped it open and shined her light under the floorboards expecting to find a telltale heart; instead she found a dented up 1968 VW emblem.

"CC, come here, come here now." Anne pointed to the hole in the floor.

CC took out her handkerchief and picked up the emblem by the edges. "That's from my VW. There are traces of green paint." CC called the sheriff's department.

They waited on the front porch in the rocking chairs. A half hour later, the sheriff from Krispy Kreme stepped out of his cruiser and came up the front porch. "What are you doing here?" he asked them.

"We came to see Catherine," Anne said.

CC grabbed her arm and hissed, " Quiet." She turned to the sheriff and said, "We came to see Catherine. The door was unlocked and there were signs of a struggle so we went inside."

"What signs?" He pulled off his mirrored sunglasses, glaring at them.

"Let me show you." They walked up the steps. She opened the door and pointed out the glass on the floor.

"Catherine keeps bees. This is a honey mason jar. I wouldn't call it a struggle," he said.

"But she wouldn't have left it on the floor," CC said.

"The sign out front says the market is closed today. There's a padlock and chain around the gate that somebody picked open."

CC became quiet. Anne kept staring at his nametag until she couldn't contain herself anymore. "O'Leary? Are you related? Catherine's maiden name is O'Leary."

CC reached in her purse and pulled out the VW emblem holding onto it with her fingertips and the handkerchief. "This is from my stolen vehicle. It was hidden under a floorboard up in Catherine's bedroom."

"What were you doing up in her bedroom?" the sheriff asked.

CC got nervous. This wasn't going so well.

"Aren't you going to make a missing persons report?" Anne asked.

"I don't know that she's missing. I do know that you're trespassing. What we're going to do now is I'm going to escort you off the property and follow you down the access road until you get back on the highway. If I find you trespassing or breaking and entering ever again, I'm going to arrest you."

"What about the VW emblem?"

The sheriff grabbed it from her hand. "I'll take that and put it with your stolen vehicle report."

Anne and CC returned to the Mercedes. Anne kept watch in her rearview mirror, noticing the sheriff following them. As they got onto the highway, the sheriff flashed his lights, a warning never to trespass in his jurisdiction again.

CC stared out the window at the summer corn, swaying back and forth in the light breeze. She had spent nearly three years restoring that VW bus from a barn find to perfection. And somebody had taken that from her. He had also taken something much more dear—Patricia's life. CC reached in her purse and pulled out the lantern key. She rubbed it in her hands. She whispered, "Come and get it."

Chapter Thirty-Two

Anne sat humming, "God Save the Queen," as she polished the 19th century sterling silver snuffbox. She couldn't believe her luck. Someone had brought it into the Treasure House where she was completing day one of her community service. She didn't recognize the hallmark right away. It was the king's head with a *G* and the initials *ES*.

She set it aside and pulled out her iPhone. She was so deep in her research that she didn't hear the silver bell over the door ping as the very tall and very British Nigel Towers ducked his head into the shop. "Hallo, Anne," he said.

"Hi, Nigel," she said.

"How's the job going, Anne?"

"Going well. I've put in two hours and I'm polishing silver," Anne said. "All in all, not a bad way to give back to the community."

"Aces, Anne; that's a great attitude to have."

"And, look, Nigel." She held up the snuffbox. "Someone donated this. If I'm reading correctly, it's an Edward Smith snuffbox from Birmingham and worth at least a couple hundred dollars. I might see if they'll sell it to me so I can resell it at our store."

"I brought what you asked for. I thought we could have lunch." He handed Anne a sealed manila envelope.

"Thank you, Nigel. I think I can get away for an hour or so. Let me check with the store manager," she said.

Anne returned shortly, snuffbox still in hand. She grabbed Nigel by his paisley tie, pulling him down toward her. She kissed him hard on the lips. "What's all this then?" he asked.

"I'm glad to see you."

He smiled and returned the kiss. "Ditto."

They walked down Pennsylvania Avenue to the small diner across the street from Great Aunt Sybil's Attic. They took a table by the window. Anne glanced out across the street. She saw Betsy Buttersworth in front of her sweet shop, waving her hands as clerks carried chocolate trays to her car.

Nigel followed Anne's stare, a bit embarrassed that they were both looking at his ex-girlfriend. Anne looked at Nigel, "We're not going to talk about that episode in our lives, are we?" Anne ordered an egg salad sandwich and homemade potato chips.

Nigel ordered meatloaf and mashed potatoes with extra gravy. As the waitress placed Nigel's plate in front of them, Anne reached over with a spoon and took a large helping of mashed potatoes. "I should have ordered that," Anne said.

"Do you want to switch?" he asked.

"No, I'll just nibble off your plate."

Anne reached for the saltshaker and Nigel put his hand on top of hers. His bony fingers interlaced with hers. "I tried texting you several times over the last couple days," he said.

"I didn't have international service," she said.

Nigel's spoonful of mashed potatoes froze in mid-air. He looked around it. "What are you talking about international service? What do you mean? Where have you been?"

"A lot has been happening. That's why I asked you for this." She held up the envelope. She took a bite of her egg salad sandwich and followed it with a large spoonful of mashed potatoes.

"Annie, where have you been?"

"We flew to Ireland to find out more about Patricia Rounder. We went to Wexford where her warrant was issued."

"Yes, I know all about the warrant."

"We went and spoke with the wife of the man who was killed. Then we took John's plane to Bletchley Park."

"John?" Nigel interrupted. "John who?"

"Oh." Anne set down her sandwich. "John Blackbear. He offered to let us use his plane."

"John Blackbear flew you to Ireland."

"Yes and England, too."

Nigel put his spoon down and stared.

"We went to Bletchley Park because we learned that the great-grandfather of the man Patricia supposedly killed worked there during World War II breaking the enigma code. He was a mechanical engineer. CC found. . ."

"So, John Blackbear went with you to Bletchley Park?" Nigel asked, interrupting.

"I'm trying to tell you the rest of the story but you keep interrupting."

"Are you seeing John Blackbear?"

"No, we broke up."

"Wait, I thought you broke up months ago."

"We didn't exactly break up, but now he's getting remarried."

Nigel pushed his plate away. "Anne, I thought we were going forward with our relationship."

"Nigel, we are. There's nothing I want more."

"I know it was my idea to take things slow. I thought it was understood while we did that we wouldn't be seeing other people."

Anne said, "I'm not dating other people. John Blackbear is getting back together with his ex-wife."

"Do you still have feelings for him?"

"I'll always have feelings for him. He was a part of my life. I don't feel that way about him now. We're just friends."

Nigel pulled his wallet out and placed money on the table. "Anne, I need to get back to work." He started to get up, bumping his knees on the edge of the table.

Anne put her hand on his arm. "Nigel, please, don't go. Let's talk about this."

"I need some time," he said. With that, the very tall and very British detective Nigel Towers left the diner.

Anne watched him walk down the street and exchange greetings with Buttersworth. Anne muttered, "Buttersworth."

She opened the envelope and pulled out the report. She skimmed it. "Entry wound, butcher knife, half serrated edges lacerating the left ventricle." She skimmed through the rest. "Traces in the entry wound of nitrogen, phosphorus, potassium, magnesium, iron, zinc, copper boron, aluminum, cobalt." She stopped when she reached the last chemical. "Molybdenum." Anne studied the chemicals while nibbling her egg salad. The periodic table danced around her head like Lewis Carroll's Red Queen's guards, but instead of hearts, the playing cards were symbols of the elements. The Queen's guards marched, forming and reforming lines; she'd never seen this combination in any of her work in all her years as a research chemist at Ebbort Labs.

She left the diner and headed back toward the Treasure House. Her questions would have to wait until her day's work was done. It was the first five hours in her hundred-hour commitment. When the several grandfather clocks chimed five, Anne raced out to her truck and headed to CC's. She tapped on the door but there was no answer. She went to the side gate, peeking over the fence. Bandit was leaping in the air catching bumblebees. Seeing the gate opened, Bandit turned and ran to the fence, barking madly. Anne pulled the gate close tight. "Bandit, it's me, Take a whiff, Boo Boo," Anne said. Bandit stuck his nose underneath the gate. A few quick sniffs and he allowed her entry. She reached down and petted his soft red and white fur. He rewarded her with a kiss of apology for scaring the life out of her.

"Bandit seems really on edge," Anne said.

CC looked up from where she was weeding her hot pepper garden. She was wearing her floppy garden hat. Nick was next to her, picking tomatoes. "He's been that way for several weeks. He won't leave my side," CC said.

"Hey, CC, I wanted to show you something." Anne waved the manila envelope.

"Give me a minute." She went over to her composter. She filled a pail and then went over and spread it over her kale garden. Bandit walked over, sniffed the kale, sneezed and then returned to his bumblebee bonanza.

"Hi Nick." Anne waved at him.

Nick waved back.

"Anne, let's go to the gazebo and get out of the sun." Following CC over to the glider, Anne sank down with a deep sigh.

"I saw Nigel," Anne said. "I got what you asked for." Anne handed her the envelope.

CC opened it and read the coroner's report. "Butcher knife? That's what Catherine was holding when we went back for the lantern. What are all these chemicals?"

"I've been thinking about that on the ride over. They're all trace minerals in soil except the nitrate is nine times higher than any soil I've tested."

CC looked down at her garden pail. There was a bit of rotten lettuce and a red worm wiggling from underneath it. "Anne, worm castings."

"What's that?" Anne asked.

"Worm castings. When used in composting, the worms break down compost, they add these trace elements and a very high level of nitrate. Catherine's greenhouse. She raises worms for their castings to fertilize her crops."

"But Catherine said she never met Patricia. That Patricia was never at the farm."

"The police found Catherine's address in the car's GPS but there was no way of telling if she was ever there," CC said. "We have to go back out there. We have to find Catherine to find out the truth."

## Chapter Thirty-Three

CC gazed out the window of the Mercedes SUV. She wasn't sure she could get used to Anne's driving and longed to have her VW back. She stuck her head out the window, checking the sky up ahead. "Looks like a storm coming in, Anne," CC said.

Anne clicked a button on her steering wheel and her nine-inch dashboard monitor flicked on. She flipped through the channels and brought up the weather report.

"Anne, keep your eyes on the road." CC glanced at the Doppler radar. The handsome young weatherman was getting very excited.

Anne turned up the volume. "Severe thunderstorm. We've upgraded the tornado watch to a warning for Grundy, Kane and Lake counties. A funnel cloud has been spotted in Rockford, heading east," he said. Anne flipped on the windshield wipers as a steady drizzle began. "CC, this is neat. The headlights have wipers."

They drove further and further into the storm, dark clouds gathering overhead, seemingly following them. By the time they reached the access road, it was pitch dark, and the rain had stopped. The sky was an eerie green. CC exchanged an uneasy glance with Anne. "I don't like the look of that," she said.

They got out of the SUV. Anne held her hand up in the air. "There's no breeze. I can smell the electricity in the air," she said.

CC reached back inside the car, grabbed her flashlight. The gate was padlocked shut. The house was dark, not even a porch light was on. "Are we going to go in?" Anne asked.

"No, I don't think Catherine's inside," CC said. She turned around and looked into the cornfields. "No, I definitely don't think we'll find Catherine inside." They walked along the perimeter of the barbed wire fence, shining the light in front of them. Anne screamed as she stumbled and fell into a deep hole.

CC shined her flashlight down. Anne was at the bottom of a four-foot trench. "Are you okay?" CC asked.

"Yes, help me up." The sky crackled overhead.

CC shined her light down along the fence. There were several other large holes. She turned her light to the edge of the cornfield. She could see more holes dotted along the prairie where it met the cornfield. "Come on, Anne," she said after pulling her up out of the hole.

They walked through the prairie, avoiding the craters. CC stopped. "This one's fresh." She shined her light on a hole big enough to be a small swimming pool. After about a mile, they stood by the edge of the woods. They sat on a tree stump.

"I'm exhausted," Anne said. "I think I twisted my ankle a bit when I fell in the hole."

Lightning crashed overhead. "We better get back to the car," Anne said.

CC shined her flashlight around the edge of the woods one more time. "Wait, Anne." She walked over. "This hole's been filled in. It's been packed down and covered with rocks. Help me move some of these."

As they knelt down, moving fieldstones from the hole, they heard a freight train in the distance. Anne turned around to the sound and then she went back to digging. The dirt was soft and easy to move as CC dug with her hands. The freight train sounded closer. Anne stood up. In the distance lightning flashed, illuminating Catherine's barn. As the tin roof went flying into the air, "CC," she called out.

"Not now, Anne, I feel something."

"CC, it's a tornado. We have to go."

"Anne, wait." CC desperately dug at the dirt. The roar grew louder and closer. The corn stalks tilted and then flew into the air. One lashed Anne, forcing her to the ground. CC shined her flashlight on an antenna. She dug further down. She could see the lime green of her beloved VW.

"CC, we have to go now. We'll never make it back."

CC clawed the dirt. With one last dig, she reached down and felt a hand. Her heart stopped. She cleared away the dirt. Lying on top of her VW was the body of Catherine Henderson. Anne grabbed CC by the back of her shirt and pulled her up from the hole. They ran through the fields as the dust swirled around, the wind forcing the corn to slash the air around them. Anne stumbled, clutching CC, as a cornstalk flew by like a javelin inches above her head.

"CC, we're lost. Where's my car? I'm all turned around," Anne panted, breathing heavily. She was cut up and bleeding from her arm.

CC covered her mouth with her blouse, trying not to breathe in the flying dirt and dust. "This way, Anne." They ran toward the wood away from the tornado. They stopped when they reached the river and the bridge. "Anne, under the bridge, we'll wait out the storm there."

Anne was shaking from her cuts and bruises. CC held her tight, putting her arms around her. "It's okay, it's okay; it's going to go right past us." The roar was intense. As the tornado passed, a whirling dervish of household items and dust and debris flew by. CC held Anne tight.

"We're not going to make it, are we? After all we've been through. We're going to die under this bridge in the middle of nowhere."

CC looked into Anne's eyes. "We're not going to die, Annie. This isn't how we die."

Anne managed a little smile. "You always know the right thing to say, don't you?"

And then silence. Everything stopped. The ringing in CC's ears stopped. A slight cool breeze started, followed by a drizzle. Anne shivered. "We're safe," Anne said. "Can we go home now?"

"Yes." They climbed up from under the bridge. A flash of yellow peeked through the debris. Lying on its side was a small bobcat excavator. CC glanced inside the cab, shining her light on the metal of its floor. Opening the door, she retrieved the lantern—the one Patricia Rounder brought to the store the night she died.

Chapter Thirty-Four

CC built a roaring fire. Anne came downstairs to the living room wearing CC's bathrobe. Ingrid brought tea and cookies into the living room. "Are you okay, Anne?"

"A few cuts and bruises. Nothing broken." Anne sat on the chaise lounge, pulling a blanket over herself.

"How horrifying for you, Anne," Ingrid said, pouring her a cup of tea.

"The sheriff's office is out there now, taking care of Mrs. Henderson," CC said.

Ingrid handed Anne a plate of warm chocolate chip cookies.

CC placed the lantern on the coffee table in the center of the two chairs. They all sat quietly, staring at it. CC pulled the key out of her purse. She carefully inserted the key into the keyhole. She slowly twisted the key to the right. The metal sleeve around the bottom of the lantern shifted, changing the shape of the Ogham symbols. And then the sleeve slowly rose up around the hurricane glass of the lantern. All three Spoon Sisters watched in amazement. CC stared at the hundreds of tiny symbols that were punched through the thin metal all the way around the lantern. She held it up under her Phoenix consolidated glass lamp. "Some of this is Ogham but it's broken up by Turingery." CC glanced over her shoulder. "Turingery is the code breaking technique that Alan Turning invented and used on the bombe machine that Patrick O'Leary helped build."

Ingrid stood up. "Look at the floor."

CC glanced down. The light shining through the metal sleeve cast faint shadows on the floor. She couldn't make it out. "Wait." She ran through the kitchen out the back door to the garage. She came back carrying a small container of kerosene. She struggled to remove the cap to the tank. She carefully examined the collar in the burner. "Anne, how old did you say this this lamp was?"

"I don't know, late 1800s," Anne said.

"No, I think it's older than that. There's no Eureka safety valve."

"What's that?" Ingrid asked, peering over CC's shoulder.

"In 1877, Robert Wetherill of Philadelphia invented the Eureka safety valve for kerosene lamps. It's a very simple piece. It's a device that's placed between the collar and the burner. It has a flat brass wing which covers a rectangular slot. The ring allows pressure to escape out of the slot rather than exploding the lamp. This lamp doesn't have one."

"Oh," Anne replied.

"We have to be very careful," CC said. She carefully filled the lantern and lit it. "Ingrid, switch off the light." The room went dark except for the glow of the fireplace and the lantern. CC carried it close to the living room wall. She took down the Thomas Kincade painting. On the wall, the light through the holes formed the first sentence. "The key to enlightenment lies down a narrow path." CC turned the lantern slowly.

"What lies down a narrow path?" Anne asked.

"The key to enlightenment," CC said. "Whatever it is we have to understand is down a narrow path on the Bee's Knees farm in Hampshire."

"What does the rest of it say?"

CC rotated the lamp slowly. "It's all gibberish."

"Patrick was a code breaker and a puzzle solver. You don't think he would have made it easy for someone to break his own code. And, why go to all the trouble of encrypting an old lantern. Why not just leave a treasure map?"

"This is a treasure map. What a better wink at the puzzle solvers than to use the mythical O'Leary/Chicago fire lantern. Like any good puzzle, he left some pieces out." CC turned the key to the left and the metal sleeve rose higher. "There's a second sleeve that's missing. Like the enigma code-breaking bombe machine that Patrick helped build, the two sleeves will line up and solve the puzzle."

"That's fine. We travel halfway around the world and find the key that fits in the lantern that was given to me by a dying woman and now you're telling me it's missing the last puzzle piece. And how are we supposed to find that?" Anne asked.

CC sat down and took a sip of her tea. She carefully extinguished the lantern.

"In one of those pictures we saw of Patrick at the enigma museum he was fly fishing with Turing. In fact, I thought there were two photos of him fishing," Ingrid said.

"Sharon O'Leary said that Patrick grew up in America." CC took out her iPhone and typed in Google Earth. She put in the address of the Bee's Knees. She opened the satellite picture. "Look, Anne, Ingrid." They both peered over her shoulder as she expanded the image. "There's a lake on the other side of the woods past the cornfields." She expanded it again, zooming in. She scanned the woods around the lake.

"Stop, look," Anne said. "Right there. There's a narrow path through the trees right to the lake."

CC swiped her finger, moving it along the path until she reached the lake.

"What's that by the path?"

"It looks like an old cabin." CC looked over her shoulder at Anne.

"I'm not going back there," Anne said.

Chapter Thirty-Five

Sassy lay purring on Anne's lap. Anne had been reading the book she'd bought at the *Downton Abbey* exhibit, titled *How to Marry an English Lord*. She closed her eyes for a minute, picturing herself in a dress by Worth, a diamond tiara on her head at court with her English lord. She had just fallen asleep when a loud banging on the front door downstairs brought her back to reality. Anne jolted awake. She looked out the window onto the street below. She checked her watch. It was one a.m. Her heart pounded as the pounding on the door continued.

She grabbed a dragon-headed walking cane and headed down the stairs. Sassy beat her to the front door with Sybil close behind. Anne peeked through the beveled glass front. She opened the door. "Sheriff O'Leary, what are you doing here?"

He didn't say a word, pushing his way inside. "Miss Hillstrom, I need to talk to you."

Anne realized for the first time she was in her nightgown. Feeling uncomfortable, she crossed her arms over her chest. "It's very late. This couldn't have waited until daylight?"

"Can we sit down, please?" he asked.

Anne walked him back to the kitchenette. He took his sheriff's hat off and sat at the table. Anne looked at the kitchen knives in the butcher-block container. She thought about Patricia and the kitchen knife that had ended her life. She backed up against the sink and put her hand behind her back touching the handle of one of the blades. "I've already given my statement. Why are you here?"

"Catherine was my sister."

Anne let go of the butcher knife. "I'm so sorry. I didn't realize."

"I believe Catherine confronted her killer with the VW emblem." He took the emblem out of his coat pocket and threw it on the kitchen table. "It's from your friend's stolen VW. My cousin, Sean, is missing. We found Sean's pick-up truck. Like Miss Muller's vehicle, it was buried on the farm. It had a mark that matched the green paint from the VW. I think Catherine confronted Sean about the VW and he killed her," Sheriff O'Leary said.

"Your cousin?"

"He served time for manslaughter. I warned Catherine not to let him work on the farm. She had a soft heart for relatives but the boy was never right in the head."

"That's horrible. But how can I help? What are you doing here?"

"He was after you and your friend for a reason. I'm here to find out what that reason is."

Anne explained about the lantern and the key and about the missing sleeve. When she was done, he repeated, "The key to enlightenment lies down a narrow path. What does that mean?"

"There's something on the farm that Sean is willing to kill for," Anne said.

The sheriff stood up and said, "We have a warrant out for his arrest." He put his hat back on.

Anne walked him to the door and locked it behind him. She stood staring through the beveled glass, making sure she saw his tail lights fade into the distance. She felt uneasy. Then she felt a tug on her nightgown. She jumped as Sybil locked her claw into the hem of her silk negligee. Anne swung around trying to catch the kitten. Sybil swung around her like a flying chair at a carnival ride. Anne couldn't stop twirling as Sybil hung on for dear life. Sassy watched from the windowsill, neither approving nor disapproving. Anne stopped and grabbed the kitten, holding her in her arms. They both turned to the portrait of Great-Aunt Sybil hanging behind the register. The kitten leapt from Anne's arms, landing on the counter. She sat quietly, staring up at the portrait, not moving. Anne walked over and followed the kitten's gaze. Anne whispered, "Yes, Aunt Sybil, I will tread carefully."

Chapter Thirty-Six

Anne followed CC along the tree line ridge. The tornado had devastated the cornfields and felled several trees. "I don't think this is a good idea, CC," Anne said.

"We're going to check the cabin. I have to know," CC replied, pulling her arm out of Anne's grasp. In the other hand, CC was carrying the lantern.

Anne trudged along, her Keds slipping in the mud from the rainstorm. They stopped at the top of a small hill that overlooked the cornfield. "It looks like a whack-a-mole game. There has to be hundreds of holes."

"Sean's been at it for years. I checked the survey plats and this farm was originally over 1,200 acres when Mrs. O'Leary moved from Chicago after the fire. Whatever Sean's been searching for, he hasn't found it."

"What do you think we'll find?" Anne asked.

"For now, we're not going to find anything unless we find the missing encrypted sleeve for the lantern. Patrick wanted whoever deciphered the lantern to work for it," CC continued. Anne followed behind her, holding onto the back of CC's shirt.

"Why go to all that trouble? Whatever's buried out here, why leave it here? Why leave it on the farm if Patrick knew where it was?" Anne said in between gasps of breaths.

"Sharon O'Leary said that Patrick left before America joined the war. He wanted to help Ireland fight the Nazis. I think that kind of man wasn't interested in personal wealth or glory."

"Oh," Anne said.

CC stopped suddenly, Anne bumping into her back, almost knocking the lantern out of CC's hand. "Careful, Anne," CC scolded.

Anne glanced up and down and saw a narrow path that led through two rows of old-growth oak trees. They looked at each other and then headed down the path. CC thought about a young Patrick making this journey before shipping off to Ireland in 1939. She thought about Patricia Rounder who had given her life to discover the secret of the lantern. She thought about Sean O'Leary, who had spent years digging and searching. She thought about Catherine Henderson, a woman who had spent her life working this land murdered and buried in an unmarked grave. CC felt the key in her pocket. She whispered, "Come get it."

They reached the end of the row of oaks and there was a lake. A small wooden pier jutted out. The late afternoon breeze slapped the water against the pylons. Facing the lake was a dilapidated wooden fishing cabin, not more than a shanty. It reminded CC of the ones she had seen on the bayou as a little girl. Rotten wood, tackle hanging on the front porch, they walked up the one creaky step onto the porch. The screen door was hanging half off its hinges. CC turned to Anne before pushing the screen door open.

The inside of the small cabin was as dilapidated as the exterior. A small table and two wooden chairs, an old wood stove, some mason jars full of preserves, not so well preserved after many years. "The smell is really bad," Anne said, covering her nose with her scarf.

A rat scurried over Anne's Keds. She screamed and clutched onto CC. CC went to the shelf of mason jars. She looked inside the small cabinet under the sink.

There were some newspapers from the 1930s. In the corner was a small table by the woodstove with a small cabinet full of fly fishing tackle and fly tying supplies. Poles leaned up against the wall. CC lifted one and felt its weight. She placed it back down. "I don't think we're going to find anything here, CC," Anne said.

By a torn-up leather chair in the window facing the lake was a workbench full of tools like calipers, renderings and a chess set. CC picked up a drawing. "Look, Anne, it looks like the Turing bombe code breaker. Patrick was definitely here." She put it back down.

"I think we're done here," Anne said.

CC nodded.

On her rush to get out, Anne tripped over a wood plank, landing facedown on the floor. "Are you okay?" CC asked.

Anne stayed motionless, staring down into the planks. She adjusted her eye to the dark. An eye from underneath the plank stared back at her. She jumped up. "What is it, Anne?"

Anne pointed to the floor. CC walked over and stared down between the planks. She reached down and tugged on one, which popped off easily and then a second. Sean O'Leary stared up at her, a bullet hole in his forehead. CC placed her hand on Sean's throat to search for a pulse which she knew wouldn't be there. "Anne, he's dead, but his body's still warm."

"We need to get out of here," Anne said as she dialed 9-1-1. "My phone's not working. There's no cell service." She backed up toward the door.

CC popped another plank off the floor. Sean was holding something in his hand. She reached down and tugged at the missing encrypted lantern sleeve. Sean finally let go. CC turned around to show Anne. "Anne, the . . ." She stopped. Sheriff O'Leary stood in the doorway, illuminated by the setting sun. His service revolver was pointed at Anne's head.

"I was the one who sent Sean to prison," he said. Anne had never noticed how menacing his eyes appeared as he held onto her shoulder, the gun pointed at her forehead.

"In 2011?" CC asked.

"How do you know that's when he went to prison?"

"He followed us into the woods at the Irish festival. He was smoking. He must have had the P. J. Carroll's when he went in early in 2011. That's the year they stopped making them." CC stood up slowly, her hands in the air. Her eyes glanced down at Sean. He looked up at her.

The sheriff followed CC's gaze, slightly releasing his hold on Anne. "Sean believed the family stories. Yeah, I thought he was crazy until Patricia Rounder showed up with the lantern. She told Sean that she was old Patrick's bastard daughter and that the lantern was the treasure map. She came hoping to find the key. When Sean said he didn't have it, he tried to take the lantern from her and she hit him with the tire iron. Tough old broad but he got her good, didn't he? And, that's when I believed the old stories."

"The key to enlightenment lies down a narrow path," CC said. "Sean figured out a piece of the puzzle was missing." She held up the sleeve.

"Yeah, the boy wasn't right but he did figure it out. I had to take care of him. He was careless and dangerous. He killed my sister."

"He was a murderer. You had to kill him," Anne said, backing away a few steps.

"Yeah, I think I could get away with that. Not too many people would question me shooting a fugitive wanted for murder."

"Take the sleeve and the lantern. Just let us go," CC said.

"Too many loose ends." He motioned with his gun for CC to stand next to Anne. As CC put the lantern on the table, Sheriff O'Leary pulled off his mirrored sunglasses. "Sean knew that the lantern was a key to finding where old Patrick buried everything but he couldn't figure out the code. And then he found the missing sleeve but it was too late; you had the lantern and the key, didn't you?"

CC nodded. Sheriff O'Leary grabbed CC by the back of her hair and pushed her over toward the table. "Let's see how this works."

CC placed the second sleeve over the first one. It fit perfectly. She lined up the keyhole and turned the key to the left. There was a small clinking sound and the sleeves lined up and rose up over the glass. "I have to light it." She lit the lantern and spun it slowly. She read out loud, "The key to enlightenment lies down a narrow path of oaks. A hundred yards east of the cabin, under the elm in a circle of ash trees." CC paused. "The elm was on Patrick's headstone and on the code-breaking computer. I thought Patrick was leading the angels down the wrong narrow path but he was leading us to . . ."

"To the treasure." A big smile crawled across Sheriff O'Leary's face. Anne huddled next to CC and took her hand in hers. The sheriff said, "Oh, no, I'm not going to kill you—yet." He pushed them out the front door and thrust a shovel at each of them. "Let's go."

Anne and CC stumbled down the narrow path between the old-growth oaks which continued along the lake. At the end of the worn way there stood a 100-foot elm in the very center of a circle of ash trees. The only elm tree in that part of the woods.

Sheriff O'Leary pushed behind them. Anne whimpered as she stumbled along the path. "Anne, I'm sorry," CC whispered. They reached the elm tree.

"What do we do now? Where do we dig?"

CC walked along the tree, running her hand along the bark. The elm was six feet around. She stepped over one of the large protruding roots. She kicked away leaves and sticks until she found the tip of a stone sticking out from the ground, no more than the size of her fist. She knelt down and brushed away the dirt and weeds. A small headstone read Daisy. CC smiled and glanced at Anne who was peeking at her. "Daisy, that's the name of Mrs. O'Leary's cow who allegedly knocked over the lantern and started the fire. Patrick had a sense of humor."

"Enough of that," Sheriff O'Leary said. "Start digging."

CC picked up the shovel and plunged it into the earth, balancing on its edge. The ground was soft. Anne joined in. Sheriff O'Leary lit a cigarette and sat on one of the big roots. Anne started crying, the tears running into the dirt with each shovelful.

"Don't do that. Don't let him do that to us," CC told her friend.

Anne stopped and wiped the tears away. She thought about Nigel. Would he be the one who found her body under this tree? She thought about Ingrid and all the lessons she still had to learn. She was grateful CC hadn't let her come. She thought about Sassy and Sybil. Then she thought about Sybil's namesake, her Great-Aunt Sybil. Was she watching? Was she trying to help? Anne looked at the lantern sitting by the headstone, the lantern that had started this whole mess. The last glimpse of earthly light she would see before she joined Great-Aunt Sybil.

CC struck her shovel and heard a metallic clank. She reached down in the hole and brushed away the dirt. She pulled out a small metal trunk. She tried but couldn't lift it. "Anne, give me a hand." They both took an end. The sheriff stood up and pulled the trunk out of the hole. He took out his folding knife and popped the lock open. Anne and CC couldn't see what was inside. The sheriff smiled and stared. He held up a handful of gold coins, letting them trickle back into the box. CC felt something under her foot. She reached down and picked up a smaller tin box. She opened it and took out a small leather notebook. She picked up the lit lantern to read in the darkening light. On the first page was a hand-drawn elm leaf. Turning the pages slowly, she scanned the list of names. Next to each one was an amount. "Anne, look at these names. Here's Palmer, Armour, Field. And, DJS. That's the chief of the fire department, he must have been in on the gambling and the cover-up. All these Chicago titans of industry owed Mrs. O'Leary money from gambling debts. This is a gambling ledger. The stories are real."

Sheriff O'Leary was standing over her. "I'll take that, too." CC handed him the ledger. He opened the ledger and started reading. "Yeah, great-great-grandma was quite the businesswoman. You know that they burnt down her farm but she escaped with the ledger and the gold."

CC understood the significance now of the symbol that had followed her from Glen Ellyn to Ireland to England and back home again. The same symbol that hung over Mrs. O'Leary's head. Her curse cast on the Chicago fire department and the titans of Chicago who burned her home and chased her out of city. Instead of angels finding her headstone she'd sent dark angels from her grave to haunt the descendants of the men who had done this to her. When CC looked up, the sheriff was pointing his revolver inches from her face. He cocked the hammer.

From out of the woods, a flash of white and red leapt onto the sheriff, knocking him to the ground. Bandit tore furiously at the sheriff's face and throat. The sheriff hit Bandit who whimpered and rolled over. He reached around the ground and picked up his revolver, pointing it at Bandit's heart.

"No," CC screamed, grabbing the lantern and flinging it toward the sheriff. Kerosene soaked his clothes, the flames burst onto his legs. He screamed. The flames traveled up his legs, catching his arms and chest on fire. The sheriff and the ledger were engulfed in flames. Sheriff O'Leary ran toward the lake, collapsing to the ground inches before touching the water.

CC fell to the ground, wrapping her arms around Bandit. Bandit whimpered but kissed her face. "Bandit, my boo bear bear, how?"

Ingrid came running out of the woods, running up to them. "Are you all right?"

"What are you doing here? We told you to stay home," CC yelled, hugging her cousin.

"Bandit was pacing back and forth, scraping at the door, growling, whimpering. I couldn't contain him. I put his leash on to take him for a walk. He pulled me to the car and dug his heels in. I tried calling you. When I couldn't reach you, I got worried. When we got to the farm and found the Mercedes abandoned, Bandit jumped out the window and circled it, growling. He took off into the woods. I couldn't catch him."

"You saved us," CC said, hugging her dog again, tears running down her face. "I love you, Boo Boo Bear," she whispered, taking his bloody face into her hands. He grinned up at her.

Chapter Thirty-Seven

Anne stared out the picture window, looking out onto the street in front of the store. She could see Buttersworth out in front of the sweet shop, arranging small café tables. She walked over and opened the window facing the sweet shop. "Mmm, lemon, cinnamon, blueberries?" She muttered. "No, I'm not giving one cent to Buttersworth. Buttersworth." She closed the window tightly and went back to her rocking chair in the front window. Sassy and Sybil jumped on her lap, fighting for position. Sassy won. Anne reached down and pet Sybil's soft white fur.

An unmarked Chicago police car pulled up in front. She could see Nigel sitting in the driver's seat, hesitating. He opened the driver's door and then closed it again, his hands back on the wheel. Finally he unfolded himself out of the car and came up the front steps. Anne jumped out of the rocking chair, opened the door and threw her arms around him. She kissed him. Nigel stood silent, steady, not returning the kiss. Anne stopped and slowly let her arms slide down his bony chest. "Nigel, I'm so sorry. John Blackbear and I are over, we're just friends. I told him that in London. I told him I could never love him."

"I believe you, Annie," Nigel said.

"What's wrong?"

"I didn't want to leave things between us as they are. I'm taking a leave of absence. I'll be gone for several months."

"Nigel, what's wrong? What's going on?"

"I have a predicament back home that needs my attention. I wanted to leave us on good terms."

"Nigel, I don't understand. Why can't you tell me what's going on?" Anne stared up at Nigel. She saw his eyes start to water. His bony cheek twinged. He kept his upper lip stiff. He looked more British than she had ever seen him. "It's a family matter of great urgency. Goodbye, Anne," he said. He bent over and kissed her on the cheek. He left.

Anne ran onto the porch, trying to think of a word, any word to stop him. She thought of three but she couldn't bring herself to say them. She felt it. She knew she had always felt those three words but they wouldn't come out of her mouth. She took out a handkerchief and wiped her eyes. As Nigel drove off, from the corner of her eye she saw Buttersworth stop her fury of table arrangement on the sidewalk and watch Nigel drive away. For the first time, Anne realized that perhaps Buttersworth did care for Nigel. That she, too, felt the pain of losing the very tall and very British Nigel Towers. Anne crossed the few feet between her and Buttersworth. "Buttersworth," Anne said.

"Hillstrom," Buttersworth replied.

"The shop looks great I wanted to say. I don't think CC and I ever officially welcomed you to the block."

Betsy stood silent, trying to figure the angle that Anne was coming at her from but she knew that Nigel had just broken her heart. "Why don't you have a seat? I'll get us some tea and muffins."

"Muffin? Blueberry? Are you making blueberry muffins?"

"I'm not making them but I have them. We've added some bakery items to our menu." Betsy stuck her head in the door and spoke in French. She sat down across from Anne. Minutes later a different young man flew out the door, carrying a tray of muffins and a tea service. "Thank you, Claude," Betsy said.

"What happened to Edelbert?"

"Claude's the new Edelbert."

Anne took a bite of the warm muffin after slathering it with butter. Betsy looked confused and asked, "Why butter?"

"Swedish," Anne said and went back to buttering the muffin. Betsy managed a small smile. "This is really good," Anne said. After Anne was done, she said. "I have to ask you. Why this shop? This block? You could open a business anywhere. Why open it next to our store?"

Betsy sipped her tea. "To be honest with you, at first it was out of spite. You had stolen Nigel from me."

Anne didn't say anything.

"But, it's more than that. You and CC are my oldest . . ." she paused searching for the appropriate word. "I've known you two longer than I've known anyone. We grew up together."

Anne thought how sad it was that Betsy couldn't say the word *friend*. "Betsy we *have been* friends a long time. We've had our differences but maybe that's something we can get past now, since we're neighbors."

Betsy raised her teacup and nodded at Anne. Anne returned the nod. It was a general understanding, a new truce settled upon.

Coming around the corner was Anne's Mercedes, with Ingrid driving and CC in the passenger seat. Ingrid pulled it to a sharp stop in front of the antique store. "This isn't the Autobahn," CC said.

"I'm still getting used to your crazy American driving rules, cousin CC," Ingrid said. "Why is Anne sitting with Betsy Buttersworth?"

CC checked her watch. "I was wondering that myself." They got out of the Mercedes and stood in front of the antique store. Anne came over to them, her lips blueberry blue. "What's going on?" CC asked.

"Oh, Buttersworth and I have an understanding now."

"That's good," CC said, happy that her two friends might have declared a truce. "I had the VW towed to my house. It's going to be my summer project. Ingrid and I cleaned it up a bit but it's going to need a lot of work."

"That's good."

"What's wrong?" CC asked.

"Nigel stopped by. He's going back to England for, I guess, a while—a long while. He wouldn't say why. He stopped to say goodbye. I think he's still angry about John Blackbear."

"I'm sorry to hear that, Anne."

Anne sighed.

"We need to sit and talk about some things. It's such a nice day. Do you want to sit on the porch?" CC asked. "We have an hour before the store opens."

Anne and CC sat in the white wicker rockers. Ingrid swung on the porch swing. "When I got the VW released from the police, they told me that Sharon O'Leary is Catherine Henderson's next of kin. I called her and she's flying out to settle the estate."

"Does she want us to have the estate sale?"

"It's a little more involved than that. Sharon is very grateful to us for everything we've done. She'll be inheriting all the gold."

"That's really great for her. Is she going to sell the farm or take it over?"

"That's the thing. She doesn't want to leave Ireland," CC said. "She doesn't want to sell the farm either because it has been in the family for so long. She wants to find a tenant or someone to work it. In fact, she would like to have us actually take it over."

"We're not farmers. What are we supposed to do with it?" Anne asked.

"She thought we could manage the store and the restaurant. We could even sell some of the honey at the antique store."

"Mmm. We could have special-event barn sales there. This could work." Anne's thoughts turned to all the large items that she'd had to walk away from because there was no room in their little store. This barn opened a whole new realm of possibilities.

"I've already thought of some great recipes for the restaurant. I thought we could fix it up and make it larger. Think of all the farm-to-table crops I could plant. Nick said he will help us. We could actually supply his bar. I think this is something we should really consider, Anne."

Anne stopped listening after "barn sale." She was in, she was already picturing the displays she could create. "This couldn't have happened at a better time. I got a letter from my attorney about my property, and it's going to be tied up in court for years. By the time I pay attorney's fees, excavation fees, court fees, I won't have any money left to build." Anne paused and looked up at her second story apartment. Sassy and Sybil were staring back down at her through the round stained glass window. For the first time, Anne thought, *What a cozy home. Why would she need more than this?* "You two don't mind watching the store this morning? I've got a lot of community service hours left. I'm supposed to be at the Treasure House in a half hour."

"Wait, I have something for you." CC pulled out a carved wood plaque. "Here. I thought you could hang this on the door going up to your apartment."

Anne looked at the beautiful rosewood carving that read, "Hillstrom Manor." "Thank you." She hugged CC.

Anne kissed Ingrid on the cheek. Then she hugged CC a second time and lingered. "It's good to be home," she said before walking down the street to the Treasure House.

Later, at the Treasure House's back room, Anne sorted through the most recent donations. A picture frame, children's clothes and old dishes. Underneath it all, she found an old cedar trunk. She opened it. Inside was a very old blue satin ball gown complete with hoop skirt, ruffled neckline and puffed sleeves. "Wow," she said. At first she thought it was a costume straight out of *Gone with the Wind* or *North and South*. And, then she examined it. Sewn into the lapel was a hand-stitched name. She read it out loud, *Isobel Grant*. Anne examined it closer, underneath the first name was stitched, "Sewn by Elizabeth Keckley." She remembered that name. She was the former slave who had become Mrs. Lincoln's dressmaker. She held the dress to her chest. She ran into the dressing room and slipped it on. She twirled in a circle as the skirt chased her. She looked over her shoulder at the mirror and twisted and turned. This was *her* dress. Then she noticed a large stain on the bottom of the hem. She lifted it up. It was a bloodstain. "Isobel, what happened to you?"

THE END

## ABOUT THE AUTHOR

With a passion for shopping, Vicki Vass drew on her experiences as an antique hunter to tell the story of her real-life friends Anne and CC. This book is the fourth in their series. The first was entitled *Murder for Sale,* followed by *Pickin' Murder,* and *Killer Finds.*

Vicki Vass has written more than 1,400 articles for *The Chicago Tribune* as well as *Women's World, The Daily Herald* and *Home & Away.* Her science fiction novel, *Eleven: 1,* was inspired by her journeys in the jungle of Sudan, Africa, while writing about the ongoing civil war for World Relief.

She lives outside Chicago, with her writer, musician, husband Brian, their 20-year old son Tony, kittens Pixel and Terra, Australian shepherd Bandit, seven koi and Gary the turtle.

www.ingramcontent.com/pod-product-compliance
Lightning Source LLC
Chambersburg PA
CBHW030309200626
46816CB00002BA/829